SANTA'S BROKEN TOY

OONA GRACE

BLURB

Mary has had enough. Enough of the comments, the looks, the eggnog. Enough of the pity she knows she'll see on everyone's faces over the loss of her husband two years ago. If no one else can move on, how can she?

This Christmas, Mary is getting away from all of that. For two weeks, her only company will be herself, a pile of smutty romance books, and her army of rechargeable, buzzy friends, out in a quiet log cabin.

But when an unexpected snowstorm closes down the roads, a handsome biker who'd caught her eye in town shows up at her door, sparking feelings that would definitely land her on the naughty list.

Apparently, Santa doesn't always show up in a sleigh. Tonight, he pulled up on a motorcycle, with a question Mary never expected:

Will you be Santa's little toy?

SENSITIVITY WARNING

Santa's Broken Toy explores themes of grief over the death of a spouse, as well as sexual healing.

Alcohol and marijuana are used recreationally (but not abused).

Anxiety and depression show up in recollection and in one panic attack within the plot of the story.

Explicit sexual content is described in graphic detail often within the story (that's what we're here for, right?) including primal play, impact play, anal play (both parties), brat play, light masochism, soft Dom/sub play, light degradation, masturbation and voyeurism.

To that punk ass tumor:
Thank you for the kick in the ovary
that encouraged me to write
the Santa smut that was in my heart.

CHAPTER 1

'm just gonna say it: eggnog sucks. That's a controversial statement, but since I'm alone in a cabin in the woods and my nearest neighbor is over a mile away, I'm not going to worry about offending someone with the truth. No need for awkward arguments about whether it's a classic tradition or just a person drinking spiced eggs in December. Nope, not doing it. Avoiding awkward conversations is the whole reason I'm spending my two-week Christmas holiday at the midpoint between east nowhere and west noplace-at-all.

"Hey, Mary, how's... work going?"

"You hangin' in there, girlie?"

"Frank and I have been praying for you. There's a reason for everything, I really believe that."

"Have you thought about getting back out there? I've got a very handsome nephew, he's in commercial real estate..."

"Must be hard, this time of year. You know, given... everything."

By 'everything', they're referring to my husband, Will, dying suddenly and tragically at age 39 two Novembers ago. Yeah, I know. There's no good segue for that one. It just... wasn't great. Still isn't.

"I can't imagine what you're going through," my friends, cousins, dental hygienists and co-workers would tell me.

But you know what? Yes, they can. They fucking *can*.

What they mean is, "I don't want to."

What they mean is, "Imagining myself in your shoes would bring me to the floor."

What they mean is, "I need to believe this couldn't happen to me. I can't *let* myself imagine it."

And that's fair. But don't say you can't imagine it. It's not an orc or a faerie, it's real life. It's happening to me, right in front of you, and it could happen to you, too. That's the reality people don't want to imagine.

For the first year, that loss, that Will-shaped hole in my chest, was everything. Every thought, every excuse, every moment. I processed every part of my day through this one cruel, inescapable fact. He wasn't coming back. To my family and friends, that loss is still my 'thing'. A label I wear around my neck.

"That's my friend from college, Mary. *Her husband died*. I know! It was this freak medical thing. I heard there was an old Grey's Anatomy episode about it, but it's very rare."

"My niece? Oh, Mary's over there, next to my nephew, Jake. You got my group email last year, right? *That she lost her husband?* Yes, yes, she is too young. Widowed at 38. It's a tragedy, it really is. Our poor girl."

"Mary? I think she's doing okay." They had one of those e-fundraisers for her. It raised a lot of money. All their friends, coworkers, everyone. Yeah, it went well. Covered all the medical stuff and the funeral. I donated a couple hundred. Of course, of course. Everyone loved that guy. Couldn't have met a better dude than Will."

It's true. It's true about how good Will was, and it's true about the money. Will was the organized one, always thinking ahead. He had it all sorted- a trust for our assets, a list of passwords, documents in a fireproof safe, and big life insurance policies.

"Jesus, Will. Why so much? Are you trying to entice me to off you?"

"It's the standard amount, Mary. 10 times a person's salary, plus enough to pay off debts. It's not excessive. It's *not*! Listen, honey. Just let me do this. We both know you'd be a mess without me. You'd need the money for therapy and a bunch of cats or crystals or dyeing your hair pink. Plus, if I die suspiciously, tumbling off some rocky hiking trail, they'll follow the money and find their top suspect. It's always the spouse."

"Psh. That gives me an easy alibi. I *never* hike, and I'll have dozens of character references to back that up."

"My indoorsy wife. I'll get you to hike with me someday. It'll happen."

Two years later I'm left with a paid-off condo in Chicago, a hearty retirement fund, financial security- all the things my anxious brain wished for except the most important one: my husband. Not having him is a deal breaker, but life doesn't deal out its cards fairly. I'd wish differently if I could, but there's no takebacks.

Instead, I finally went on a hike with Will. I huffed my way up a steep hill and spread some of his ashes off the side of the path, down the rocky hillside.

"Well, we're on a hike, Will. Better late than never," I told him with a bitter, teary laugh. "And if anyone finds you here like this, they won't suspect me at all."

It's been a bleak couple of years. This past year was both easier and harder than the first. The world kept spinning after Will died, even though it had stopped for me. But this year, after a solid twelve months of grief, I had no choice but to hop on for a spin, too.

The Will-shaped hole hasn't gotten any smaller, but life keeps getting bigger around it. The amount of my story post-Will keeps growing by the day. I even quit my job to give myself a break, to maybe try writing. It's a dream I've always had, this fantasy existence of drinking coffee and telling stories all day, of letting my creativity out to play.

It took losing Will to realize that the real fantasy is a practical, safe life where nothing bad happens. I always forced myself to be practical, play it safe. Never daring to take that leap, to jump and find out where I'd land. I was still too scared to jump off that cliff, if I'm being honest. Instead, I'd been volunteering around the city, trying to focus on helping others. Even though nothing can fix my situation, I hoped, maybe, that I could make someone else's better.

Annoyingly, all the damn books, blogs, and inspirational quotes on Instagram were right. It actually does get easier with time, bit by bit. I can go hours, sometimes nearly a full day without my heart bottoming out in my stomach remembering he's gone. Lately, I've even passed couples on the street, and I think not about what I lost, but what it'd be like to have that again. With someone new. I'm considering what the future will look like not for *us*, but for *me*. Just me.

Those little daydreams worked, for a while.

Then, earlier this fall, my need for human companionship started complaining. Loudly. 'Just me' wasn't cutting it anymore. I did what seemed easiest, letting friends and co-workers set me up on a few blind dates.

Spoiler alert, I wasn't ready, and it didn't go well.

Small talk with a stranger is nothing like small talk with your husband. Will knew my history, my tone, my body language, the entire subtext behind an innocuous statement like 'I saw toucan guy at the bus stop this morning' or 'Sherri finally put in her notice today, can't wait to see what Bald Rob has to say about that'. Trying to read all those nuances in a stranger's words, each response a potential landmine, was too much to handle. Especially when comments would trigger memories about Will, and I'd end up apologizing while tears fell into my cacio e pepe. At the conclusion of those failed attempts, all I ended up with was a few doggie bags of leftovers and several awkward conversations with friends about why their cousin/co-worker/accountant was nice, but not a love match.

Clearly, diving straight into real life meetups was too much, so I downloaded a couple of dating apps. I'd scroll through them in bed, 'meeting' men via their profile instead of a Friday night reservation. Will and I were together 15 years, before dating apps became common. We met the old-fashioned way, drunkenly colliding into each other at a friend's Halloween party. So, it was very new, this feeling that there was a laundry list of men out there for me to consider. And frightening. Because that also meant there was a laundry list of women for them, women with less complicated, less tragic backstories. The whole thing was intimidating.

Still, I'd lie in bed, swiping through pictures of Jake, 42, Environmental Engineer. Jake with a big fish on a line. Jake with a dog (is it his dog?). Jake smiling on a beach with a couple of kids (are they his kids?). And then, Jake, smiling in a selfie, looking straight into the camera. A twinkle in his eye that made me wonder. Wonder what the 'environment' in his bedroom was like. Wonder how capable he was of 'engineering' up some orgasms for me.

I'd hold Jake in one hand, snaking the other inside my pajama pants. As an experiment, of course. Was Mary, 40, Writer, ready to sit across the table from someone new? Was Mary, 40, Widow, ready to lie underneath a stranger? Because Will, forever 39, wasn't here. And Mary, 40, still was. I'd spasm against my fingers, mouth open in a silent yell, staring into the eyes of a stranger through my phone screen, feeling like a stranger myself. I felt guilty for doing that to Jake, 42, fishing enthusiast and possibly father. I felt guilty for doing that to Will, 39, dead.

Dead. He wasn't here. Isn't here. Won't be, ever again.

Unfortunately, to everyone else, he *was* still here, as *me*. A big, red WIDOW tattooed on my forehead. And I just couldn't do it again, another Christmas of the looks and the pity and the platitudes. My favorite holiday turned into a one-woman traveling show, the WIDOW on display at the work party, the family dinner table, the boozy gathering of college friends at the bar. One after the other, weekend after weekend, all filled with awkward conversations with the people who love me, who loved Will. Well-meaning loved ones who expect me to simultaneously grieve forever, while also moving on and being happy.

No. The widow show is cancelled this year. I'm opting out.

That's how I ended up in a remote cabin in December, drinking eggnog because it was the first bottle I grabbed from my alcohol crate (yes, crate). But, as I mentioned, it's gross. The festive display at the grocery store had steered me very wrong. So, that's not the best start. I was hoping a drink would warm me up a bit before I had to unpack everything from my car, but I don't think I can stomach a full glass of this stuff.

My arms shiver in the drafty cabin, so I walk over to the fireplace and get the fire going. I need old-fashioned heat since the alcohol won't do its job. My fire-starting skills are rusty, so it's probably better I do this sober, anyway. The rack next to the fire has enough wood for the evening, but in the morning, I'm going to have to go on a mission for wood. Like, timber. Not like…dick. It's not that kind of trip.

Once the fire's going, I give the cabin a once over. It's dusty and needs a thorough cleaning, but I'd crossed my fingers that it would be devoid of memories, and luckily, it is. Will inherited this place from his grandfather, but I've never been here before. We'd talked, hypothetically, about fixing it up, but never got around to it, another item on our list of dead plans. Now, it's mine.

The cabin's been vacant for over a decade, so I hired a man named Vern off Craigslist to come check everything out prior to my arrival. The last thing I needed was to have no running water or electricity and have to drive four hours back home from Michigan. Vern responded to my email in all caps and used a lot of words like lintel and damper casing, so I assume he's much older than me and about a hundred times handier. His last email said, GOOD TO GO, MA'AM, so I promptly sent him a check, which I had to search through several drawers to find as I prepared for my getaway.

The cabin is a proper log cabin; the walls built of golden, knotty wood. Most of the floor is wooden planks, except for tile in the kitchen and bathroom. The kitchen, dining room, and living room are all one open, cozy space, and in the back, two bedrooms sandwich a single bathroom.

One of those bedrooms is full of boxes, some older, aged ones belonging to Will's grandfather stacked behind the boxes Will stored here forever ago when we moved in together. It's all so old and unused that I have to imagine there's nothing triggering tucked away in those plain brown boxes, but I shut the door anyway. It's a Pandora's box I'll open when I decide to, but not today. Maybe never.

The other bedroom has a rustic wooden bed, dresser, and two nightstands. They could be handmade, but neither of the men who'd know are available to ask. A chest sits at the foot of the bed, filled with plaid sheets, old quilts, and Pendleton blankets. The slightly musty, mothball smell coming from the chest makes me glad I brought my own pillows as I make the bed. There's a small side window framed by plaid curtains. I consider shutting them, but the window faces out to the side of the property, and the stars look beautiful, so I leave it for now.

My last stop is around back, so I throw on my boots and head out the door. As I walk around the house, I cross my arms over my chest as goosebumps cover my skin. It was chilly when I arrived, but the wind is picking up now, whipping the cold air against me. I turn the corner quickly and head for the covered hot tub. The cover splits in the middle, so I lift one side up to see clear, steamy water bubbling away. My hands clap involuntarily. *Thank you, sweet baby Jesus and sweet old Vern.* I was crossing all my fingers and toes that this old hot tub would still be functional, so as I watch the crystal-clear water stream out of the jets, my spirits lift. The hot tub overlooks the forest behind the house, and I've been dreaming for weeks of a soak under the stars with a drink in my hand. The garage is across the gravel drive from the hot tub, blocking anyone from seeing it from the road.

"Okay," I tell myself with a clap of my hands, "this'll do. This'll do just fine."

I'm going to have a good two weeks here. It's not my style, per se, but I vibe with this place. We've got a lot in common, this little cabin and me. She used to bustle with life, filled with love, but it all died away. She sat dormant for a bit, stuck in limbo as the dust settled around her. But now we're both here. Sure, we're both fixer-uppers, but we've got a lot of life left in our bones. With a little time and effort, we'll clean up nicely.

I spent two months daydreaming about how I wanted this trip to go, and there's no time like the Christmas present to make it happen.

First step: get very high.

CHAPTER 2

hadn't actually planned this step. I'd packed clothes, booze, a dozen smutty romance novels, and some buzzy toys. Everything I needed for two weeks of self-care. Emphasis on *self*.

On the way here, about ten miles south of the cabin, I stopped for gas at a state road intersection. A half dozen shops littered the area, spread across each corner of the road. A gas station, a country store, a pharmacy, a tiny diner- all the normal places for a no-stoplight town, and I'm being generous with the word 'town'.

As I pumped gas, I noticed a cottage-style shop with cute white shiplap siding, and a hand-painted sign that read 'Milk & Cookies' in an exaggerated script. I assumed it was a little coffee shop or bakery. Since caffeine and sugar are my two main vices, I had to stop in. I crossed my fingers that their coffee was good, so I could make this place my daily outing into civilization. Bells chimed overhead as I pulled the heavy, black wooden door open.

I stepped inside the little cottage, and immediately the smell was all wrong. If this earthy, musky smell was any representation of their coffee, I was in trouble. Walking up to a display of baked goods, I noted the prices were above average and the case was locked in the back. Confused, I looked up at the chalkboard menu on the wall and realization swept through me. Instead of coffee and tea, the sign listed a variety of strains and prices per gram. Was this a dispensary? I knew there were recreational dispensaries in Michigan, but I didn't expect them to look like this. How... *random*.

To put the nail in the coffin of my confusion, at that very moment a man walked through a curtain from the back and into the shop. A quick scan revealed his plain white t-shirt, black jeans, and if my glimpse of his feet was correct, motorcycle boots. He had an impressive number of tattoos per square inch, covering most of his visible skin from his fingers to his neck. This biker was someone's ideal fantasy man, but a bit too young to be mine. He was young, muscled, and mildly dangerous looking, and I was... forty.

Overall, I'm comfortable with myself. Each year older I get, I seem to lose an equal number of viable eggs and fucks left to give. Good riddance to all of it. But I also know what I'm working with, and what I need. Will had been the type of man I needed. He was an accountant: stable, diligent, and eternally optimistic. At heart, I'm a creative; easily inspired and prone to whimsy, but also prone to fits of seasonal depression, panic attacks, and doomsday levels of pessimism. Between the two of us combined, Will and I used to joke, we made one mostly functional person.

Standing in this shop, staring at biker boy, I wasn't sure what percentage of a person I was, but not a whole one. Definitely not ready for the man in front of me, with his buzzed hair and hard lines of muscles under his shirt.

I knew all of that was true. I was *not* ready, and he *was* too young, but it still didn't stop me from imagining the way his stubble would feel scraping against my inner thighs as his tongue explored where they meet.

Wow. Well then, Mary.

I guess I'm glad my libido hasn't totally died with my husband, at least. Although, to be fair, I'd probably need to get my hormone levels checked if someone like dispensary guy didn't give me *any* flutters downstairs.

The man coughed purposefully, bringing me out of my fantasy and back into the empty, quiet dispensary.

"Can I help you with anything? Sorry I wasn't out front when you came in, I was just getting the store opened. Rarely have any customers this early."

I glanced down at my phone in my hand. It was 1 pm.

"It's fine, I'm going to need a minute, anyway. I saw your shop sign, 'Milk & Cookies', from the gas station. I thought this was a bakery or something."

"Yeah, you and every other middle-aged white lady driving through."

"Ouch," I responded, turning away from him to hide my grimace, but I still caught the way his eyes started to widen as he realized what he said.

"Fuck. I mean. *Shit*. I didn't mean that. You caught me before I finished my coffee and fully woke up. I was just trying to say, you're right. The exterior doesn't match the business inside. This backward-ass little town has a lot of strict regulations on building design. Every-thing needs to fit in with the 'aesthetic of the neighboring structures'."

"So that's why this place looks like it should be owned by a little old lady with white hair serving cookies, or maybe a millennial serving artisanal cupcakes and oat milk lattes?

"Exactly. I don't see how it's better to confuse people into acciden-tally entering a shop full of weed. Anyway, this is what you get instead. A dude in a dispensary. We have cookies, though. All of them baked with 7.5 mg of high-quality THC infused in the butter. Standard dose is one or two, depending on the person."

I looked over the options in the case. My standard cookie dose was an entire sleeve of something chocolatey and crunchy while watching home improvement reality shows. THC not included.

"Pot Peanut Butter? Cannabis Chocolate Chip? Sativa Sugar? Cute."

He groaned. "I'm just the manager, okay? I *am* running new ideas by the owner, though, but he likes the rhymes." He seemed legiti-mately frustrated over the cutesy names.

I couldn't help it, I laughed. The kid looked like he was barely old enough to drink. You'd think this would be a dream job, but he was acting like a toddler one step away from a tantrum. Something about him rubbed me the wrong way, the same thing that bugged me any time I was in the presence of someone who had a good thing and didn't seem to realize or care. No one seems to realize they're living the dream until they're thrown out of it. I guess that's something we all must learn with age, and he's surely not old enough for a life lesson like that.

"How old are you?"

"What the hell, lady?" he sighs, running his hands down his face. "I don't see how that's important, but I'm twenty-two. Old enough to work here, if that's what you're asking."

"I see." Twenty-two. I was already out of high school when he was born. Lady boner successfully killed, although his petulant attitude had already done 80% of the work there.

"It's too early for this shit," he mumbled to himself as he rubbed the sleep from his eyes and turned to me, speaking at a normal volume again. "Listen, I'm gonna grab my coffee from the back. I'll be here when you decide what you want. Or you can sneak out while I'm gone, I won't be offended."

Obviously, he viewed me as some old, vanilla white lady, but I wasn't so old that I was going to hightail out of there without buying some of those cookies. I bought one of each flavor cookie and left the under-caffeinated biker alone.

Dispensary guy thanked me for my business, but he mostly looked thankful I was leaving. Good riddance, kid.

This kind of interaction is exactly why I'm spending the next two weeks alone. No strangers, no awkward conversations. Just me, my books, and my booze. And now, my edibles. I walked out the door, paper bag in hand, toward the crosswalk to get back to my car. I heard a loud, rumbling engine and looked up, expecting drag racing punks with their mufflers removed, like we get in Chicago.

Instead, I stared into the deep blue eyes of a handsome, older biker as he pulled up to the stop sign. My mouth dropped open slightly as I realized he was looking at me too. Surprised by the intimacy of his stare, I dropped my gaze down, taking in his large leather and chain boots, black jeans that stretched over thick thighs, and a zipped-up leather jacket. As I trailed back up his body to his face, there was a shit-eating grin nestled in his thick salt and pepper beard.

My jaw had been slowly dropping, rational thought fading into fantasy, but that smile shocked me back into the moment. I almost lost my grip on the paper bag, so I pulled it up to my chest and cradled it in two hands. The biker revved his engine at me, his sharp-eyed smile cutting deep into my psyche. He extended his left hand to signal a turn, his two gloved fingers pressed together, then winked at me as he veered left and pulled into the Milk & Cookies parking lot. Whether my cheeks flushed pink, or it just felt that way, he had rattled me, and those two fingers unraveled me completely.

Standing frozen on the corner, hugging my pot to my chest, I thought about those two fingers pressed together, imagined the places they could go and the things they could do. The wavering thoughts I'd had about the sour biker in the store were conspicuously absent as I'd looked over this man's body like a feast I'd wanted to dig into. I had the distinct impression that had he patted the back of his bike, I'd have hopped on and rode off wherever he was going.

It unsettled me.

I'd spent fifteen years knowing exactly what I needed, and suddenly that notion had evaporated like an exhale in the cold air. If I couldn't have what I needed anymore, what exactly did I want? And why did I have the strangest suspicion it had inky blue eyes and biker boots?

No. I'd faced enough loss. A man like that was too far out of my risk profile, too far outside of anything I'd experienced in my life. If I went home with someone like that- someone dangerous, someone unpredictable, I'd be the one to lose. He'd take what he wanted, and while I might enjoy the way he touched me in the moment, there was nothing to come of it long term. It would inevitably end exactly where I'm standing now, alone on a street corner as he drove away. A fun fantasy, but a tragedy in my life, a life that had already seen too much of that.

Still, as I headed down the gravel road back to the cabin, mouth watering for the cookies on the passenger seat next to me, I tried to remember if I had packed any biker romance novels.

CHAPTER 3

The cabin isn't huge, so within a couple of hours, I'm done cleaning and high as a kite from two delicious cookies. I listened to Taylor Swift as I cleaned, singing along loudly to her newer, folksy albums. The cottage core vibes fit the whole 'woman alone in the woods' thing I'm going for. All I need is a flowy white dress and to run barefoot through the woods. And, you know, for the temperature to be above freezing.

Now that the place is clean, I'm finally ready to drag my stuff in from the car. The garage sits back from the house and across the gravel, but there's no back door to the cabin. When I got back from Milk & Cookies, I backed the car up to the front door so I wouldn't have to walk up and down the gravel drive from the garage multiple times.

If it keeps snowing, I should probably see if my car will fit in the garage, but with the sun already set, I don't know if I want to investigate in there. This is exactly the type of job I would have made Will do. I have no clue if the garage is empty, full, or home to a family of possums. Right now, I'm too high to deal with surprises.

I'd probably end up lying on the garage floor playing dead too, I think with a laugh as the snow starts to really come down.

Weird. There wasn't any snow on the forecast for this weekend.

Still, weather can sweep in quickly in this part of Michigan, gathering steam as it crosses over the lake. By the time the last of the laundry baskets are inside, the temperature has dropped significantly, and the snow is falling in sheets. I watch as it melts on the gravel, thinking how it'll all turn to ice by the time the sun sets.

The clock reads a quarter til six, and right on time, my stomach rumbles. I completely forgot to eat lunch, so all I've had since arriving were the two cookies. Looking over the groceries I packed, I just don't feel like cooking anything. I'm a bit too loopy to figure out a new stove, anyway. I grab a pre-made salad from the fridge instead and settle down at the dining table. As I chomp my way through the salad, I think about the 'woman laughing alone with salad' meme and giggle hysterically to myself. The exaggerated smiles of the stock image women juxtapose absurdly with the image of me right now, sitting alone in an empty cabin, eating leaves. I laugh so hard I snort. God, it feels good to be high. I haven't done this in a long time, and I forgot how nice it is.

I clean up my dinner and then look around the house, trying to figure out what to do next. It comes over me suddenly, this mood shift that often occurs at night. A wave of melancholy pours in now that I'm out of tasks and distractions. Even the calm melodies playing from my portable speaker contort into something else, the folksy chords plucking at the strings of my sadness, vibrating through me. They settle into my darkest corners, the shadowy places that remind me happiness can only last so long.

I go to throw a couple logs on the fire, but there aren't that many, so I just take one. As the new wood crackles and pops, I flop myself down on the old plaid couch. I'm at a decision point I've arrived at many times before, standing on the edge of an emotional cliff. Do I let myself fall into the pit of despair, let the burn of memories singe me like the licks of flame rising in the fireplace? Or do I pull back, throw cold water on my lonely pity party, and find a new distraction?

You are one melancholy little sad sack right now.

How many times will I let myself sink into this place? It's been two years of this, pleasant conversations and happy days ending with this lonely pit in my stomach. Ever since Will died, it's like my heart is too broken and my brain too shocked, neither one of them capable of captaining this sinking ship. All the memories, all the hopes and dreams drag me underwater, and there's no one left to pull me out.

Fuck. If I was a little sad sack before, I'm at least a medium/large now.

If I wanted to be a sad sack for the holidays, I'd have stayed in Chicago. I'd have sat across from my mom at her faux marble dining table and let her pity-filled stares bore into me. Pretended to focus on a football game so my friends didn't feel obligated to ask their cautious questions about how my life is going. I'd have watched everyone shush my five-year-old niece after she asked me 'why did Uncle Will die and not you', while I asked myself the same damn question. One particularly sad thing happens to me, and I'm doomed to make everyone around me sad too.

I let out a sigh.

Fuck this.

I didn't come all the way here to live out the same shit as home. I stand up, backing away from the cozy fire. The owl clock on the wall reads 7 pm, and I confirm it with my phone. I've got plenty of evening left, and my high is dying down, but it's still there. The buzz helps me separate myself from my feelings, at least by a couple degrees. I grab a bottle of peppermint schnapps from my crate, twisting the cap open and skipping the step of making hot chocolate. Taking a swig, I let the confusing sensation of warmth from the alcohol swirl with the spicy coolness of the peppermint on my tongue.

I walk purposefully to the end table, sifting through the stack of smutty books I'd set there. Holy shit! I brought a biker romance. As I pick it up, I realize that it's a big, thick, book.

There's a sex joke there, just waiting to be made.

Nah, I'll save this one for another day. I don't have the patience to wait for the tension to build. My fingers are twitchy, and I can't wait until 65% into the book for the characters to fuck. I need less plot, more porn. Instead, I find the wrinkled spine of one of my favorites, an anthology of dark fairytale erotica. I attempt to pull it carefully from the middle of the pile, but my coordination is far too impaired, and the stack topples to the ground. Eh. Oh, well. That's morning Mary's problem.

Heading into the bedroom, I throw the book on the bed and rummage through the laundry basket I'd haphazardly 'packed' my things into. The tote bag I'm looking for sits tucked to one side, a black canvas bag with the words "SMUT SLUT" screen printed on the front in red letters. It was a gag gift from Will that I rarely use, but it felt right for this trip. It's only me up here, so there's no one to judge, anyway. Untying the straps, I dump its contents on top of the dresser and spread out my collection of eight sex toys so I can easily find what I want.

I'm not a deviant or anything. I used to have a great sex life, but now, like everything else, I'm alone in that too. All the responsibilities fall on me now, including getting myself off. That's not always easy to do when you're sad, so I've outsourced the job to this little collection of rechargeable independent contractors.

I choose the purple rabbit vibrator and a bottle of lube, then settle under the covers with my toy and my stories. I begin my one-handed reread of a Beauty and the Beast story, then The Twelve Dancing Princesses, then Rapunzel. It's hard to read when I'm high, so I rely on my imagination to fill in the gaps of these stories I know so well. It's all good, but I can't get myself there, cresting over the wave into great.

I keep picturing Will. Will climbing my hair to a tower, me griping at him to stop pulling because it hurts. Will following me to a castle, watching me dance the night away while he stands to the side. By the time I hit Will as the grumpy Beast, I give up. As good as our sex life was, masturbating to my deceased husband is just not doing it.

Frustrated, I turn to the clock on the nightstand. 7:45 PM. I decide to switch tools, and head to the dresser to pick something new. In the last half hour, I've stripped down to an old t-shirt and panties, the rest of my layers lying discarded on the floor. Sweat beads my skin from exertion, but it's cold out of the covers, making me shiver involuntarily.

I select a different vibrator, one I bought just for this trip. It promises a new 'thrusting technology', which, yes, please. For all the headaches men cause, it's hard to find a suitable replacement for a nice cock and a man who knows how to use it. *My kingdom for a sexy man between my thighs*, I plead, wishing on the bright stars shining through the window. Hmm. Fairy Godmother smut. Maybe I should try writing that.

I place my thrusty new friend on the bed, needing to use the bathroom before I try again. Just as I'm finishing up, there's a loud knock at the door. It surprises me so badly that I fling the toilet paper roll I was holding into the air, the paper unspooling like I'm trying to T.P. my cabin.

I wipe quickly, silently freaking out.

Who could it be, the cops?

Why would the cops be here? I'm being paranoid.

Maybe it's a murderer, but do murderers knock? Wouldn't they be standing in the window under a spotlight in, like, a fucking mask or something?

Was there even a knock or did I just hallucinate it?

Jesus Christ on a cracker, I am very high.

As I walk tentatively toward the door, I catch myself just in time to realize I'm still in my underwear. Rushing back to the bedroom, I grab the first pair of shorts I see in the laundry basket, plus my oversized fleece robe. There's another set of knocks at the door, slightly louder this time, thus confirming this is real and I'm going to have to do something about it. I fling on the robe and head up front.

If this is a murderer and I die here, alone and orgasmless, I'm going to be really pissed off.

I stumble, tripping as I work my legs into my shorts on the way to the door. Once I'm back on my feet, I take a deep breath and grip the doorknob. It swirls in my vision, making me suddenly aware that I'm more drunk and high than I thought. As I look downward, trying to get the knob to stop moving, I also note that my shorts are extremely tight. And, well, short.

Fuck.

The second I open the door, a bitterly cold wind whips in, striking my bare skin. I wrap the robe around my body as I look up, gasping on an inhale when I see who's in front of me, standing on the gravel at the base of my concrete front step. The doorframe sits a foot above the ground, so normally I'd have to look down slightly, but he's so tall we're eye to eye.

Jingle my bells, how fucking high am I?

My sexual frustration and THC-infused brain seem to have conjured up a hallucination, because the biker from the intersection is standing at my doorstep. I find myself caught in his penetrating blue eyes, pulled in like a magnet the same way I'd been earlier today. Feeling exposed, I clear my throat.

"Um, hi. Can I help you?"

"Good evening, ma'am. Just had a problem with my…" He seems to focus in on my face, his eyes flaring with recognition as he takes me in. "Wait. Didn't I see you in town earlier today?"

He scans down my body slowly, and there's a glint in his eyes I can't quite place, but it feels like more than recognition. Was that a smirk?

"Bit cold out for that kind of clothing," he states, either flirting or judging.

I feel myself shiver from the combination of the icy wind and his gaze on my bare skin. My brain swirls, unable to decide how I feel about his statement, but I land on annoyance, since it's a much less complicated emotion than attraction.

It's not like I was outside shoveling in this. I'm a grown woman, and I can wear whatever I want. If I wanted to open the door in a bikini and a pair of cowboy boots, that'd be my choice to make.

I let out an annoyed huff before responding, "Well, I'm perfectly dressed for the company I was expecting."

That company was a series of fictional men and a rechargeable imitation cock, but he doesn't need to know that.

A huff of a laugh leaves his lips. "Touché," he responds with an amused smile. Something about making a big, tough man like him laugh gives me an intoxicating thrill.

He legitimately is big, I confirm, taking a moment to really look at the man in front of me. He's tall and stocky, and the way his biceps threaten the integrity of his studded leather biker jacket makes it clear he has muscles under there. Below his jacket, he's wearing black jeans that are obscenely tight at the thigh over studded boots with a chain on each side.

He's older than me by a significant amount, and it looks good on him. His hair is predominantly white, with just a sprinkling of peppery gray running through it. The top of his hair is slicked back, windswept but somehow flawlessly styled. His neatly trimmed beard, more salt than pepper, partially obscures the sharp line of his jaw.

His eyes smolder at me from behind his aquiline nose. I imagine his muscles underneath those stiff clothes, and that image does more for me than any of the fantasy men in my books. I feel heat building in me despite the cold, a glimmer of a thought in the back of my brain that he might be capable of finishing the job my battery-powered friends failed to complete earlier.

Welp, there it is. New kink unlocked. Not only do I have an age-gap fantasy, now I need my fantasy man to look like a hot biker Santa, too.

Focus, Mary. Focus. There's a man you just met on your porch, and you are alone in a cabin in the woods. This is how an episode of "My Favorite Murder" starts.

Shaking myself out of my thoughts, I realize I've been silent for a bizarre amount of time. My only explanation is my current THC level, but I don't feel like getting into a discussion about what either of us were doing at the dispensary earlier.

"Sorry," I state, pulling myself together. "Where were we? You knocked on my door, wearing a lot of leather. According to *your* calculations, I don't wear nearly enough. I think that's about where we left off. Now, back to my original question. How can I help you?"

He gestures behind himself to the motorcycle parked at the front of the gravel driveway, his mouth open to speak, but my eyes narrow as I cut him off.

"Actually, wait. We saw each other in town, and now you're here. Are you following me?"

His brow furrows. "There's one road in and out of town, and this is it."

Lord have mercy, his voice. Low, husky, and highly disorienting. Like a spiderweb, it'd be so easy to get caught in the intensity of it.

"What's your point, that it was easy to follow me? Because that wasn't my question."

A lock of hair falls into his face, and he tosses his head to move it back in place. I feel my core flood at the silver fox James Dean move, suddenly forgetting what we were even talking about.

"Listen," he rasps, "the roads are shit, and I started hearing a bad grinding sound. I needed to stop, and this cabin was here. Didn't know it was yours, although it's mostly crusty old men out in this area, so I can't say I'm disappointed."

Given that the last owner of this cabin was Will's grandfather, he's not wrong.

I search his face, trying to figure out if I'm safe or not. I might frustrate him a bit with my cheeky retorts, but it seems clear he's not a weirdo or predator like I feared when I first heard his knock. No, if anyone is the weirdo, it's me. A high-on-edibles middle-aged woman who gets lost in lengthy conversations in her own head. A woman who will absolutely use her thrusty new friend to explore her shiny new kink as soon as he leaves. Still, it's probably best to stay on guard.

"I don't know, seems like too big of a coincidence. Kind of creepy. I've seen plenty of horror movies that start just like this."

I've also seen plenty of porn that starts like this.

He stares me down with an intensity that makes me question whether I thought those words or spoke them out loud. An increasingly insistent part of me wants to say it, to flirt with this man and see how he reacts.

"Are you saying I look dangerous?" he asks, his voice rumbling through me as I slide into my own little fantasy again.

Shit. He *is* dangerous. The feelings he's stirred up in this short amount of time can't possibly lead to anything good. My body tingles when I think about it, but I tell myself it's just the cookies and the cold. I can't let him get to me, so instead I make myself feel annoyed that he's interrupted my night alone with my collection of silicone.

"It's late. What do I need to do to get you off my porch?"

"Wasn't on it," he replies with a subtle grin, then steps up onto it, sticking his hands in his pockets in a bold challenge that says, '*it's your move*'.

We're on equal footing now, but I feel more off balance than ever as he towers over me, his gaze boring into me. I try not to react, to appear unaffected, but my panting breath exposes my lies, and my hardened nipples confirm exactly how much my body wants him up in my personal space. He flicks his eyes down to my chest, his lips curling in amusement, and I pull my robe closed to cover the evidence of my desire.

For the second time today, I fantasize about what it would be like to have a biker's face between my thighs. The idea seemed silly earlier, when I was still sober, so I should probably assume it's still a bad idea. I look back up at him, trying to think of a snappy response, but I realize he's been standing there with an amused grin on his face, watching me think.

"No response?" he quips, stepping back off the concrete. "Let's start over. Hi. I'm Samson," he says, holding out his hand.

Shit. I really wish my brain was braining better right now. His words whirl around in my head.

Not possible.

"Santa??"

CHAPTER 4

"Did you say your name is *Santa*?"

I scan over him again. His white hair and white beard, his red cheeks. It's probably from the cold air whipping his face at high speeds on his bike, but that's not where my brain goes at the moment. A red shirt peeks out from under his biker jacket, just over his black leather belt with its large silver buckle. I look down at his outstretched hand, and then back up to his face. It all fits.

His mouth turns up at the corner with a surprised little huff of air.

"I absolutely did not," he replies, his words tinged with a trace of amusement. He watches my eyes as they dart back and forth between his and he sighs, combing his white hair back with his fingers. He shakes his head as his lips curl into a small smile.

"Let's try this again, like we're at a spelling bee: Samson. S, a, m, s, o, n. Samson."

"S, a, m, s, o, n," I reply, wincing at the slight slur to my S's. I'm annoyed at him treating me like a child, but also frustrated with myself for being unable to keep up with a normal conversation. I don't care if it's been half a day, I blame it on the eggnog.

"What were you, I mean..."

Good one, Mary, great start.

I try to string words together, but his chiseled features cut right through that string, causing all my words to glide off it into a useless heap. Blinking a few times, I try to regain focus.

He is just a man. I can talk to a human man. Even if he is absurdly hot and I'm absurdly high and schnapped up.

I take a deep breath, then say in a pitch that's much squeakier than I hoped it would be, "So, what were you doing all the way out here again?"

He huffs out a curt laugh. "Delivering presents to good little girls and boys."

His deadpan words are clearly a joke, but my body throbs with desire when he says "good little girls" in that gravelly voice. Clearly, those words are out of context, and my libido's response is out of pocket. Yet, for the first time in two years, in this of all places, I want to push. I want to play, despite all the reasons I shouldn't. What I *should* do is call him an Uber and get him out of here now.

"You won't find any good girls here."

Fuck, what am I doing? This is exactly what I decided not to do, but I seem to be thinking with my pussy instead of my brain. I'm playing with fire.

Or making a fool out of myself.

The cool air whips my hair against my face, and I reach for the hair tie at my wrist, pulling my hair up with both hands. Unfortunately, this causes my robe to fall open again. His penetrating gaze trails up the inside of my robe, pausing at my too-short shorts, and then settles on my chest. The freezing air blasts through my thin shirt, and I'm not wearing a bra. My nipples are so hard they could probably function as headlights to guide him back to the road, but he stares at them like they're bullseyes. After a few lengthy seconds, he moves back to my face.

Maybe I'm not misreading this. That didn't look like the stare of a man desperate to get out of here.

No, Samson, there aren't any little girls here, just a lonely woman whose thoughts one could only describe as bad. Filthy.

"I'd still have a job to do," he replies, his voice like smoke on the air. "Naughty girls need coal. They need a punishment to remind them how bad they are."

Fuck me sideways, this man is trouble.

His eyes widen in surprise, and I'm 90% sure I accidentally just said that out loud.

Fortunately, he breaks out in a hearty laugh, the tension dissipating with each solid "huh, huh, huh". His forceful laughs blow the steam of our breaths between our bodies, and I watch them swirl together in a heady mist. I imagine the way the steam would shoot out from between us if I launched myself at his lips right now.

It's so hard to focus when I'm this pent up from not being able to get off. As I wrap my robe around myself, I focus on making my face as serious as possible, begging my cloudy mind to clear up for just a few minutes.

"Listen, Santa."

"Samson," he corrects, with a wisp of a smile.

"Samson," I sigh.

Jesus, get it together Mary.

"So, your motorcycle is on the fritz? I'm sorry to disappoint, but I'm not a mechanic."

"I would never have guessed," he says jokingly. "And to answer your question from earlier, I drive by here most days on my way home."

"On a motorcycle?" I ask, looking behind him at the snow gathering on his bike. "Doesn't seem smart."

"It isn't. This storm came out of nowhere. It's nasty."

Are you nasty too, Santa?

"I'm experienced enough to drive in this weather, but a gear started grinding. Got any tools back in that garage?" he asks, his head nodding toward the back of the drive.

Right. Garage. Whatever strange flirtation is happening here, he's just trying to get home. He doesn't want to use my body; he wants to use my tools. The realization that part of me *wanted* him to have followed me here slaps me like a whip of stiff wind. My hands ball into fists, frustrated that two cookies and a few shots has me thinking about throwing myself at the first man who shows up at my door.

I blame it on the eggnog.

I shove my hands in my pocket, not wanting him to see how on edge I am right now. My mind jumps to a dozen different places at once. The place he *should* go is home, but I'm starting to get tired of all the shoulds. Unluckily for him, I have nothing to service his motorcycle. His body, though…

Stop being a horn dog, Mary.

"Sure. It's my first night at this cabin, though, so I don't know if there are any tools out there. Don't even know how to use the garage door yet."

"You're not the most helpful little elf, are you?" he teases with a crooked smile, his cheeks rosy from the cold.

"I'm too tall to be an elf," I respond, unsure whether I'm flirting at this point.

"What a shame," he replies. "You'd look cute with the ears."

So, we're still flirting. I hope my cheeks are red enough from the cold that they hide my blush. Too flustered to retort, I let the silence linger long enough to veer into awkwardness again.

"Okay," he coughs. "Any outside lights on this cabin?"

"Unfortunately, I know as much about the lights as I do about the garage. I know nothing, Jon Snow."

The joke falls flat.

"Jon Snow? I thought I was Santa?"

"It's a quote, kind of. He's a character in Game of Thrones. He's like this sexy, scruffy, bearded warrior guy."

STOP. TALKING. MARY.

"Huh. I've heard of it. Never seen it," he answers, clearly unable to follow my train of thought, which, to be fair, I'm barely following either.

"Never? How old are you?"

Crap. That was rude. Whatever filter I used to have, I clearly left it on the counter next to the cookies.

"Fifty-five," he answers, unbothered. "I don't watch a lot of TV, though."

He looks good for fifty-five. Great, even. He has *muscles*. I would have thought that a fifteen-year age difference might be too much for me to continue my little biker Santa fantasy, but it only makes it better as I imagine his salt and pepper beard scratching against my skin in unmentionable places.

"I didn't mean it that way. I was just curious."

"Curious," he repeats, letting the word settle in the air. "I'm curious about something too. May I?" he asks, gesturing in my direction. I nod, just barely.

I freeze as his arm moves, his stare locked on mine. Whatever game I'm playing with Samson, I want to win. Just as he comes so close his arm might touch my body, he reaches across his chest into the cabin, feeling along the interior wall. I look to the side, following his hands, remembering those two gloved fingers from earlier.

I finally realize what he's doing when his fingers find the light panel to the left of the door. He moves from left to right, flicking each switch down and then back up with those two fucking fingers. When he hits the middle switch and the interior light goes off, my eyes shut with a heavy exhale. God, the things I imagine him doing in the dark with those fingers. When he flicks the switch back on, my eyes fly open. He finally flicks the last switch. Nothing. None of them turned on any lights outside, but having him this close sure as hell turned me on.

He steps back, and the haze of desire becomes less thick the further he moves away. "Okay. No lights outside," he says.

I attempt to sort through these feelings burning within me. A stinging lash of shame for reacting so strongly to Samson, this stranger, this person who is not my husband. The desire for Samson to burn that guilt out of me, to send these thoughts so far away that, for even one night, I forget all the reasons to say no.

"Option B. Can I borrow your phone to use the flashlight? Mine's dead."

I come down from the clouds, all my lust and fantasies clattering back to Earth again. He's still trying to leave, and I should let him. I *will* let him. I'll help him until his bike is working and he's driving back out of my life.

"Sure, let me grab it."

I tie my robe shut, knotting it as I walk to the kitchen. Grabbing my phone from the counter, I bring it back to the door and turn the flashlight on.

"Thanks," he answers with a dip of his head as he reaches for the phone, but I hold on to it. His head tilts quizzically as his hand stops in midair.

"Let's get you out to the garage to look for those tools. Whatever it takes to get you back on the road so I can get back to my... book... faster."

I quickly slip on the shoes I left by the door and start walking back to the garage without inviting him to follow. I can see the confusion on his face as I walk past him.

"Why're you so interested in the garage?" he asks flatly.

Because you're *going there.*

"Need to keep my eye on you," I reply curtly, hoping he can't read all the ways I mean that. "And I haven't been in there yet. Maybe there's room for my car, if it's going to keep snowing like this."

His longer legs have caught up with me, and I see him nod, accepting my thin explanation.

"So, what're you up to out here?" Samson asks, making small talk. "Haven't seen any signs of life out of this cabin for years."

"Just wanted to get away for the holidays, spend some time alone. Well, I was trying to," I say, acting put out. He ignores that part.

"Away from what?" he turns to me and asks. His face is open, and he looks sincerely curious. For all his tough clothing and intimidating size, he seems genuinely nice. Nothing about him is setting off warning bells or striking me as dangerous. He can't see my face behind the beam of light, and I'm grateful for small mercies as I bite my lip. This is a bad idea, I remind myself, steeling my resolve to not sink further into this attraction.

"From people. And their questions," I answer, more sharply than I intended.

His brows furrow, but then he nods, his body tensing as his demeanor shifts.

"I'll take care of this as quickly as I can. Shine the light here, please," he says pointedly, then motions toward the bottom of the garage door.

When we reach the garage he squats down, causing his legs to splay outward. I shine the light at the bottom of the garage door, but it's like I've turned a spotlight on his crotch. I turn my head away before I get sucked into the light like a bug in a zapper.

His hands feel along the bottom lip of the door. It's not locked, so when he tugs up, it rushes into its slot along the ceiling of the garage. With the door out of the way, the light from my phone fills the space. There's a lot of equipment in here, too much for my car to fit, but there is room for Samson's motorcycle. He finds a string on the garage ceiling and tugs, causing a lightbulb to flicker on.

The light from the garage illuminates the driveway as well, and I watch as he heads to his motorcycle and throws his muscular leg over the seat. He unlocks something on the handle and then he's using his powerful legs to walk the bike toward the garage. His quads flex and release, powerful enough to move hundreds of pounds of vehicle with his thigh strength alone. After he manipulates the bike into the garage, he swings his leg off, landing himself well within my zone of personal space.

As I inch back from him, my ass hits against a workshop bench. Samson stands there, engaging in another little stare off, and I give him my least friendly scowl. He looks frustrated, running his hands through his hair, and I hope he doesn't see the way my eyes widen as I watch him. Something about his gruff, annoyed attitude works for me too. This growing lust doesn't seem to have many limitations.

"Since you don't like questions, how about I just guess out loud?" he growls as he surveys his motorcycle.

"Fine," I answer, feigning a fiery annoyance despite the way my body is burning to get closer to him. "What do *you* think I'm doing out here?"

"Well, right now you look grumpy as fuck. You're out here alone, but this garage is filled with shit that I can't imagine is yours. Am I wrong?" He looks tense, but it doesn't look like pure frustration.

There's something else, a pressure building between us. A challenge.

"It's not my stuff, no," I concede, not like that proves anything.

"Well, then he must have either cheated or never existed at all, and you rented a random cabin all by yourself. Either way, you seem lonely as hell. Based on how intoxicated you look, I'm gonna go with... cheated."

Well fuck you, Santa.

I thought the pressure between us was about to drag our bodies together, but instead it's fuel for the bomb that sets off within me at his assumptions.

"Yeah, that's exactly what you'd see, isn't it? A middle-aged woman couldn't possibly want a vacation by herself. Couldn't be content, happy, satisfied. No, obviously the only reason I'm here is because some man left me."

Samson stands up from his squat next to his bike and moves in my direction. His eyes are dark as he closes the distance between us in one powerful stride, placing his hands on either side of my hips, caging me in. I can't decide if I want to slap him or grip his wide shoulders and pull him into me. He's still tense, coiled like a predator. Why is that even hotter?

Is this happening? Is this a horror movie or porn?

"Don't put words in my mouth, little girl," he growls deeply. "I said I thought he cheated, not that he isn't a fucking imbecile for doing it."

I just told him I'm middle-aged, but he when he calls me little girl, it throws me off balance. I like it. My knees shake as he closes in on me, the edge of the workbench pressing sharply into my lower back.

"Oh," I respond softly, "I see."

His face softens at that, his jaw relaxing as he studies me like a question he needs to answer.

"Whatever it was, you didn't deserve it." His jaw tenses again, like he'd punch someone for me if I asked. I can't tell if it's about me, a stranger, or he just likes a fight, but I enjoy the idea that he'd protect me.

His chest is millimeters from my face as he lifts his hand, and I brace myself for whatever he's about to do next. He reaches over me, the leather of his jacket brushing against my face for the briefest of moments, and then he plucks a tool off a hook behind me and returns to his bike. Suddenly my whole body is on fire, my chest flush with heat as the feeling of leather against my skin still burns on my cheek.

Jesus Christ, myself and Joseph. Porn. Definitely porn.

I need some space away from this man.

"Well, I'll, uh, leave you to it," I mumble, pulling my robe tighter, covering where it had gapped open at my chest. "I'm gonna make some coffee. You want any?"

"Black," he replies, his gravelly voice scraping along my ears. With his intense gaze on me, I feel it everywhere, these jet-black intentions swirling between us. His eyes bore into me, and I feel pulled to admit all my darkest desires to him. Instead, I rush inside the house and shut the door, pressing my back against it as I try to calm this fire within me.

CHAPTER 5

The coffeemaker I find looks dirty and old, so I use the French press I brought instead. It takes several minutes, and I spend all of them lost in a fantasy, picturing Samson in the fairytale stories from my book. It's Samson climbing the tower, gripping my hair, my back arching as my head tips back with a soft moan. The pain at my scalp and the promise of pleasure at his hands unravel me as he climbs through the stone window casing into my tower prison. Then, Samson following me in the inky night, his boat trailing behind mine, watching me dance from a shadowy corner of the ball until his hand whips out to grab my wrist, pulling me into the shadows with him. I feel my heart rate increase, the blood rushing to my clit.

Holy shit, I feel like I could come. I rush back to the bedroom, throbbing with desire. Alone, I let myself sink into these feelings. I grab my bullet vibrator and thrust my hand into my shorts, pressing the toy against myself with a loud moan. Backing up to the bed, I sit on the edge, spreading my legs open to press more firmly against my clit. The fantasy rushes in, and it's Samson the Beast, all claws and fangs as he throws me on the bed like an animal. He towers over me, fully in command, fully owning me. My other hand grips the quilt, my thighs quivering as my orgasm explodes out of me.

My eyes remain closed as I come down, waiting for my heart rate and breathing to return to normal. When I finally open them, my jaw falls in shock as I stare straight into Samson's hooded gaze through the garage window. Oh god, how much of that could he see? I'm frozen in his stare as I watch what looks like the curl of a smile form on his lips. Darting forward, dying of embarrassment, I pull the curtains closed. Once they're shut, I slam my back against the wall, taking a few steadying breaths before I turn to peek back through the curtain. When I do, Samson is no longer at the garage window.

I realize I still have a hand down my shorts, so I yank it out, then turn the vibrator off and fling it on the bed in remorse. Why does he make me feel so reckless? Straightening my clothes, I speed walk into the main living area to look out of the window there, but there's no sign of Samson. Briskly, I head to the window on the other side of the fireplace, but I can't see him from there either. The light is on in the garage,-and I can make out his bike, but he's not in there with it.

I can't imagine he fled into the woods, but maybe I freaked him out so bad that he just started walking? Flinging the front door open to the frosty night, I find myself face to face with his large, leather-clad chest. I take a startled step back, both surprised and unsure what to do next. Pretend nothing happened? Try to joke about it?

"Can I use your bathroom to wash up?" he asks calmly. If he was affected by what he saw, he's not showing it. Maybe I hallucinated him. Can weed do that? "Also, is it ok if I use your phone? I can't get this fixed, so I need to call someone to come get me."

Backing out of the way, I point him to the bathroom. After he walks past me, I focus on taking deep breaths to calm myself down. My heart is still racing from the intensity of my orgasm and being caught afterward. It could have been mortifying, so I'm grateful for his lack of comment on whatever he saw back there. Pretending it never happened works just fine for me.

Samson exits the bathroom and moves to the kitchen counter where I'm pouring two mugs of coffee. He nods his thanks as he takes the one closest to him. I sip at the scalding hot coffee as I slide my phone over to him and watch as he enters a number, then holds it to his ear. In the quiet cabin, I can hear the tone from the phone's speaker as the signal drops. He redials, but it quickly drops again.

"My phone doesn't get a signal in this area, and it looks like yours doesn't either," he states.

Nervously looking up from my coffee, I try to predict what solution he's about to propose, but his face is blank. When he catches me watching, his eyes trail down my body again, making his jaw tense. I can't tell whether he wants to run up to me, or away from me. My nerves rattle around in my chest.

"Okedokey, artichokey," I respond with a trembling, fake enthusiasm. "Give me a couple minutes to drink this coffee and clear my head a bit, and then I'll drive you wherever you need to go."

"What's your name?" he inquires, throwing me off guard.

"Mary."

"Mary," he repeats, my name rumbling out of his lips as he speaks it for the first time. It sounds like sin. "You can't drive tonight, Mary."

I chug a large sip of my coffee, grimacing from the scalding liquid.

"Don't be silly," I answer too brightly, grabbing my purse off the island and pulling out my keys. He's right, and practical Mary would agree, but she is conspicuously absent tonight. I don't know how much restraint I have left in me, so I need to get him out of the cabin and into my car quickly.

Samson places his large hand on top of mine, caging my fist and the keys against the countertop.

"Infuriating, stubborn woman," he grumbles, the gravel in his voice skidding against my last threads of self-control. "I'm not letting you kill the both of us when I could just as easily walk."

I'm the one who's infuriating? Um, absolutely not. I didn't ask for any of this, for him to show up tonight with his sexy, dangerous voice, his sculpted body, and his dominant energy that makes me want to push boundaries. In fact, I was totally fine until he threw my whole day in a tailspin. I might not be acting like it lately, but I'm a woman of action, and the action I choose to take is to drive him far, far away from me.

Yanking my hand out from underneath his, I walk briskly to the door. Just as I'm turning the handle to step outside, his large palm splays against the door, pushing it shut.

"Stop, Mary. I'll walk."

His body leans over mine, his palm bearing down on the door just above my shoulder. As I turn around to face him, I startle as I realize how close our bodies are.

"You can't. You'll freeze," I respond breathlessly. I was going for breezy, but the heat of his body sucks all the force out of my words.

"Look, Mary, it's obvious you had plans for some kind of a night, and I barged in unexpectedly. I'll be fine, okay?"

My only plan was to get wrapped up in the idea of a fantasy man and get off, and he made that happen for me. Even if I can't drive, I can't let him wander into a snowstorm, either.

"Y-you won't," I stammer. "It's not safe."

My palm opens, releasing the keys from my grip, and they drop to the floor with a clanging finality as all the fight drains out of me. Samson and I lock eyes, our breath syncing up in some kind of sexual tension showdown. All of this, the closeness of our bodies, Santa knocking at my door, it doesn't feel real. I want it to be, though, so badly I can taste it. My eyes trail to his pillowy lips, and the fantasy sweeps me under, all my inhibitions floating out into the snowy night.

My previously limp arms shoot up around Samson's neck as my body presses against his stiff, functional clothes and the sculpted muscles underneath them. His lips still, frozen against mine. My eyes fly open in response, taking in his unblinking shock. I pull back immediately, flinging my body into the door with a thud, unable to flee because of the way he has me caged in.

"I'm so sorry. I don't even know what came over…" I begin, but I'm cut off by the force of his arm wrapping around my back, drawing me into him with a curse. His mouth descends to mine, taking control of the kiss I started, then deepening it as he grips me by the waist and crushes his hips against me. His lips claim mine, his skillful tongue devouring me as I sweep against his with equal hunger.

All my desire and fantasies spill out into my limbs as they take on a life of their own. My hands and legs move in a frenzy as they latch onto him, pulling myself up to him with my hands on his shoulders, my legs circling his waist as I practically climb his body. As his hands grip my ass, he pulls me into him, and I feel his hard length for the first time. He backs me into the door and settles his hips between my thighs, the pressure of his cock making me moan involuntarily.

When I bite down on his lower lip he shudders, my body mirroring his with its own shiver of desire. He makes sure my body is secure against the door before he pulls his face away from mine. I awkwardly attempt to follow his lips forward, wanting to stay enveloped in his kiss. One of his hands grips my throat, pinning me against the door with it.

"Wait," he commands.

My brain spins, immediately self-conscious of the way I scaled his body like a feral animal. I haven't done anything like this in so long, and I'm not exactly thinking straight.

"Are you sure you want this? Because as soon as I get inside of these tiny fucking shorts, I won't be able to stop."

I feel a flush of warmth that he's checking in with me, although I initiated this. I consider his question. Do I want to continue down this path? I feel him trying to stay still until I answer, but as he steadies my ass in the grip of his large hand, he presses himself against me again. My pussy responds, clenching around nothing. I nod my head yes.

He tightens his grip on my throat with a quick squeeze.

"I need to hear you say it."

"Yes," I squeak, every nerve in a frenzy from his grip around my throat.

He bends down, his breath against my ear sending a tremor through my body.

"Beg."

"Please," I moan obediently.

"Please, who?" he asks, the corner of his lip tugging upward mischievously.

"Samson, please."

His hand tenses against my throat again as he shakes his head.

Fuck.

"Please, Santa. Please, fuck me."

CHAPTER 6

"Santa is so damn ready to play with his little toy," Samson growls.

He grips my thighs as he carries me to the kitchen island. My core floods at the idea of being his plaything. He sets me down on the edge and makes quick work of removing my robe and t-shirt. Every part of me is under his control, from his plundering tongue to the way his hands glide over my body, like he's surveying a new land he just conquered.

His thumbs swipe over my nipples, making my back arch, thrusting my chest closer to him. As I release a needy moan, his mouth immediately drops to my breasts, swirling his tongue around the hardened peak on the left before sucking the right into his mouth.

How did I forget how good this feels, how much I need this feeling?

Samson works my breasts so efficiently and expertly that my dizzy brain can't process the sensations fast enough, leaving me no space to worry or over-analyze, just to feel. I've spent two years waiting for things to feel right, to feel ready for this step. I don't know if this is right or wrong, but I know I don't want it to stop.

The cabin is drafty, sending alternating breezes of cold air and heat from the fire, confusing my nerve endings and spreading goosebumps across my arms. When Samson strokes his hand up my arm to hold my cheek for another deep kiss, he feels them immediately, reading my body and responding right away.

My mind flashes to all the grimaces I have to play off as smiles at the holidays, the way my posture sinks further and further with every well-meaning but hurtful comment. It feels nice to have someone notice when I'm uncomfortable. Samson picks me up and walks us closer to the fire. My bare torso and breasts press against the cold leather of his jacket, making me gasp as my nipples harden to little pebbles. I see his eyes flick down to them again just before he lowers me onto the plaid couch by the fire.

When Samson's hips settle between my thighs, I immediately tug at his jacket, wanting his skin against mine. My hands rush over his body in a frenzy. Now that this is happening, I want all of it immediately. The way his body is hard in all the places mine is soft has me delirious with need. I imagine the ways his hardness could bruise me, impale me. I get the sense that whatever happens, Samson will leave his mark on me, a physical bruise, maybe, or something deeper. Just as my mind acknowledges that worry, he reaches back to pull his shirt off, revealing a chiseled physique covered in tattoos. All rational thought instantly tumbles to the floor with the red fabric.

For all his hard muscles and bold tattoos, Samson's gaze in the fire-light is soft. The way his eyes wander over my body is reverent, delighted even. There's something steely in there as well, dominant and demanding, but I realize with some shock that he likes what he sees. His solid frame nestles between my thighs, and my lip quivers as the hardness of his belt and his cock underneath settle against me, blocked only by my thin shorts. Guided purely by my wanton hunger, I wrap my arms around his back, digging my nails into his shoulders as I pull him closer.

"Please," I beg.

Samson sits back on his knees as my nails scrape along his sides in protest with a needy whimper. His fingers tunnel beneath the stretchy waistband of my shorts, and my hips rise obediently, allowing him to make quick work of removing my shorts and underwear, dropping them into the rapidly growing pile of clothes.

"These little fucking shorts, they've been driving me crazy since you opened the door."

As soon as I'm fully bare, he clutches my legs against his hips, groaning in approval of his unimpeded view of my wet core.

"What do you want, little toy? What do you like?"

I'm immediately overwhelmed by the question. The man hovering above my naked body might look dangerous, but it's clear that tonight, Santa is here to deliver pleasure. The only danger is giving him more than my body, but I know better. I know what this is. Tonight, I want to let go, to take whatever pleasure is on offer. I answer his question by lifting myself quickly from the couch and pushing his torso back into a seated position. He groans as I move to straddle him, dipping my head toward his lips and spreading them open with my tongue. His metal belt buckle is cold against my slit, a strange sensation that I lean into, rubbing myself up and down against the metal, letting my instincts guide me.

Samson growls at the movement, steadying my hips in a bruising grip as he pulls his face back from mine.

"Nuh uh, little toy. I asked you to tell me, not show me," he rasps. "I'm playing with you tonight, not the other way around."

Samson drags me up with him until my feet land on the floor. He kicks the end table away, replacing it with my naked body as his palm bears my torso down over the arm of the couch. I turn my head toward him, my eyes hazy with lust as I watch him remove his boots, belt, jeans, and then briefs. He stands there with the sculpted body of a god, and for a moment, I'm intimidated again. He strokes his large, thick cock in his hands, up and down, staring at my vulnerable body.

"See something you like, little toy?"

"Y-yes," I reply shakily.

"Let's see if you're ready for it, then."

Samson strokes his hand over my ass, squeezing each cheek possessively, and I feel my arousal drip down my inner thigh. His fingers trail down the seam of my ass, then between my legs. He curses when his fingers discover how wet I am, his lips releasing a deep, rumbling groan. Sweeping my arousal up and down along my pussy, he spreads it over my clit in lazy circles that have me melting into the couch.

"Fuck. So wet for me."

Moving from my clit to my pussy, he breaches my entrance slowly but firmly. The thickness of his fingers stretches me open, and the strain is almost too much. My upper body lifts off the couch, hands flattened on the cushion to steady myself as he slowly thrusts his fingers in and out.

"Relax, Mary," he commands, and I bristle.

Even though he's right, I do the opposite of his command, using my arms to counterbalance my hips and thrust back onto his fingers, enveloping them inside my needy pussy. Although I love his dominance, a part of my brain wants to keep some control, to use his body for my own pleasure.

I'm his little toy? No. He's my big one.

Samson snarls harshly when I move, shocking me with a firm, sharp smack to my ass. The sting only serves to work me up further, my pussy growing used to his fingers, allowing me to thrust against him even harder. I hear his rough grunts, reveling in the power I possess, the way he's losing control before I've even touched his cock.

"I see you, little toy. I see the way every part of you is waking up to my touch."

He slaps my other ass cheek, the sharp sting transforming into a pleasant ache, releasing endorphins that drive me wild. His fingers curl into me, stroking along my walls until they find the spot that has my pussy clenching and legs shivering involuntarily.

"There she is," Samson says as he continues stroking my g-spot and I whimper loudly.

I feel the familiar pressure building, but it's stronger than usual. I can tell it's going to be intense when I come. A trembling moan escapes as I remember how I came with my vibrator, with him in my fantasies. His hand snakes around my front, circling my clit with firm pressure, and I scream suddenly, the pleasure from his fingers better than anything I could've imagined. I fasten my eyes closed as I ride the steep hill of the roller coaster, my whole body anticipating cresting over to the other side, when Samson abruptly removes his fingers from my clit and my cunt.

I wail, thrusting myself back against him, clenching my pussy around nothing. He spanks me again, and I'm so close I almost come from that alone.

"You're not following my directions, naughty little toy. Are you going to be a good girl, or are you getting coal tonight? Because I can stop any time I decide."

I whimper in frustration, my whole body begging for release, needing him to just fuck me already. My exasperation rises as he silently waits for my response. I want to push back, challenge him, but not as much as I need to come.

"I want it. Please," I respond, my body going soft and pliant. His hand strokes down my spine, feeling the way I've submitted, the lack of tension in my muscles.

"Mm, much better," Samson praises, his voice scraping through my ears, igniting my desire.

I hear the rustle of his jeans and then foil tearing. His fists brush against my ass as he works the condom down his length, and I respond with a pleased hum. His head finally brushes against my entrance, and I exhale a deep breath of relief as he smooths it along my slit. I grasp the couch cushion in my fists to keep myself from moving, desperately trying to be patient. Not that he'd know, but I've been waiting, needing this, for longer than I think I even realized.

"This is what you want?" he rasps.

A filthy, strained moan clears my lips as I nod eagerly, and then he's finally entering me, sinking his thick length into me in smooth, slow thrusts. I suck my teeth as his width stretches me with a deep, burning ache. He stops when he's fully seated inside of me, gently stroking my ass as he gives me time to adjust, setting off a new wave of arousal. After a moment, he restarts his movements, easing in with small, gentle strokes until I'm moaning sweet little cries with each push. Once I've grown used to his size, he pulls almost fully out, then plunges back in with one rough stroke. He lets out a guttural grunt as he seats himself fully, and I hear the satisfaction in his deep groan as he does it again and again.

He works my body expertly, his perfectly angled strokes following a steady pace that sets my body on fire, and I have a strange moment of jealousy. Samson and I only met today, but he fucks me like he can read my body like a book, the type of precision that can only come from experience. In my fantasy the man knows exactly what to do, I remind myself, and the moment of jealousy passes as he pulls my hips upwards with his hands, delivering pressure against my g-spot that has me keening with pleasure.

Thank you, ladie(s), whoever you are, for teaching him how to pleasure a woman like this.

The fireplace crackles as Samson stokes my orgasm higher and higher with each powerful thrust. I feel his hips stutter, his rhythm breaking as his fingers curl tighter on my hips, and I can tell he's getting close.

"Rub that little clit, Mary. I want you coming around my cock before I come."

My fingers follow his command, sweeping figure eights along my sensitive, swollen clit. I focus more on my own desires than his command, delirious with how fiercely I need to come. My moans turn short and breathy, then wail louder and louder as Samson's deep grunts crescendo with mine, his hips stuttering wildly but continuing to thrust rapidly until I come first.

As I tip over the edge with a wild, powerful scream, my legs shake with the force of my orgasm. My clit throbs, pulsating against my fingers, my pussy clenching around Samson's cock until he comes with a deep roar, locking my legs against the couch with his weight. His release erupts, the force of his body pinning my fingers even more firmly against my clit, surprising a choked sob out of me as a second wave of my orgasm crashes through me. When he's done, Samson's body goes limp over mine, his arms holding himself up on either side of my torso as he steadies himself, his heartbeat thumping against my skin.

When he pulls out of me, I feel empty and slightly cold without the heat and weight of his body.

"I'll be right back," he whispers as he walks away.

From the back of the house, I hear the bathroom door open and shut with a snick of the lock. The empty feeling fades as I lay there, resting my cheek against the couch cushion, grateful for a few moments to recover. Closing my eyes, I lose myself to the sated feeling in my body, the calm after the battering storm of Samson's cock. My body relaxes into the couch as my mind attempts to process the events of the last hour.

CHAPTER 7

lift up from the arm of the couch and sink into the soft couch cushions, a satisfied smile curling my lips. After two years of grief and worry, it feels like I've ripped the band-aid off to find myself more healed than I thought. It'd been a disservice to look at sex through the lens of a new relationship, something serious and emotional. Maybe I'm so wired for monogamy that it's obvious to everyone else, but I'm just now realizing that it doesn't need to be that complicated. I can get the things I need physically without all the baggage of a bigger commitment. I'd been on dating apps searching for someone to take Will's role, but maybe I just needed to find someone to roll around in bed with for a night.

Realization floods me with guilt.

I haven't slept with anyone since Will.

Well, that's not true anymore, is it? I did, and worse, I want to do it again. Trying to wrap my head around the fact that I had sex outside of my marriage sours my stomach.

Will and I had a good sex life. That's not a brag, and it's not me kidding myself. We both wanted each other equally and enthusiastically. Some mornings I'd get down on my knees in front of him while he was sipping coffee and take him in my mouth. Some evenings he'd sneak under my blanket on the couch, eating me out while we watched sitcom reruns. We'd joke about how I was going to develop a Pavlovian sexual response to laugh tracks, that I'd end up flooding my panties whenever I heard canned laughter.

We knew what worked for each other, and there was comfort in someone knowing my body that well. Will knew exactly where to touch me, exactly how I'd react. Occasionally, he'd surprise me with a night at a hotel in the city, and we'd fuck against the window fifty stories up, the entire city lit below us. I'd buy random sex toys to try and we'd either laugh through the experience (a strap-on) or find out new things about ourselves (a butt plug).

Sleeping with the same person for fifteen years was a stabilizing factor in my life, something I could always count on. Given that I wasn't making the smartest decisions in my mid-twenties, it continues to shock me that I found and chose such a stable, loving man at twenty-five.

Over the course of our relationship, Will probably slept with three different versions of my personality and four or five versions of my body. He always, without fail, told me how beautiful and sexy I was. Eventually I started believing him, mostly. I always believed *he* thought I was beautiful. It was day-to-day whether I believed that about myself as well. When he died, it was hard to determine if that belief continued to be true, or if it was Will-specific.

Now, as I'm lying on a couch after being fucked senseless, I try again to determine how all of this makes me feel. Does it feel like cheating, even though it's clearly not? If Samson tried for another round and I said no, would I be cheating *myself* out of an experience that might be good for me? He's a beautiful man who probably could have anyone he wants, and for tonight, he wants me. When he looks at me, there's none of the pity I fled here to escape, just lust. He sees a woman, not a widow, and I like that. So, I should let myself have this, right?

I hear the sink turn off in the bathroom and I sit up straight, not sure what happens next. As I adjust my position on the couch, I glimpse my naked torso. My stomach creases in the middle, displaying two rolls of fat. My D-cup breasts rest a couple of inches lower than they used to, slightly flattened and spread out. Gravity has stolen the perky lift they had back in my twenties. I shift into a new position to paint a prettier picture, but now I can see the stretch marks on my hips and cellulite on my thighs. Looking around for a blanket, I panic as I realize they're all in the chest in the bedroom.

I decide to grab one before Samson comes out of the bathroom. I tiptoe like a not-so-little mouse, only to be stopped in my tracks by the muscled wall of Samson's backside in the doorway to the bedroom. Apparently, my critical thoughts were so loud that I couldn't hear anything else, including him finishing up in the bathroom. I make a fake coughing noise to alert him to my presence. He's far too large for me to scoot around him, so I wait as he turns to me with a satisfied smile and mischievous glint.

Samson makes room for me by walking over to my dresser, his fingers running over the selection of sex toys laid out there. He turns toward the bed, eyes lasering in on the toy I used while he watched from the garage.

"I'm a big fan of these," he says casually, lining up the toys on the dresser in a neat line.

"Sex toys?" I ask, surprised. I thought they intimidated men, especially this many little soldiers in a row. Most women probably had a couple, but I had a frickin' army.

"Mhm," he confirms. "You have good taste in sex toys, Mary. Expensive taste, too. Which is your favorite?"

Another question that startles me. It feels personal, raw even, to reply to an intimate question like that. I scan my collection, trying to determine what my answer would even be. This is exactly the type of conversation I've had freely at the adult store when I go in, so why not tell Samson? He's a stranger, too. It's not like I'm going to see him again after the storm clears.

"I usually like the suction one," I answer semi-confidently. "But I just got this rabbit, and I have to say, I'm pretty intrigued about the thrusting part."

Despite the conviction in my reply, I feel my nakedness acutely, like I just ate a forbidden apple in the Garden of Samson. I quickly open the chest and pull out a crocheted blanket, wrapping it tightly around myself.

Samson frowns. "Why did you do that?" he says, his voice a mixture of concern and authority.

I quaver, even less interested in exposing my emotions than I am in exposing my naked body. Still, I don't know if he'll keep pushing or get the hint. He backed off in the garage, a bit. Still, I can't just ignore his question.

"Listen, Santa's little toy isn't shiny and new, okay?" I answer hesitantly. "This toy has flaws. Stretch marks on my hips, saggy tits, cellulite, the start of some wrinkles," I explain, my hands tracing over my face. "It's been a while since anyone took this toy out of its box, and a lot of years since someone new played with it. Now that we're done 'playing' with it, I'm putting it away, which is my decision to make."

I feel my chest and cheeks flush red as Samson's eyes trail up my hips and breasts to my face, tracking the flaws I mentioned. His head tilts like he's trying to figure me out, and it makes me nervous. This isn't the simple, easy fantasy I want.

"Who said we're done?" he asks, his body language full of intent. "Anyway, your body felt great to me when I was fucking it. Looked great, too. Why are you wasting time imagining flaws, little toy?"

I stumble away from him a step, taken aback by his assessment. It was one thing to be naked earlier. I mean, it's pretty hard to have sex if you don't at least have the essential bits uncovered. But to pretend my 40-year-old body is tight and unblemished is borderline cruel.

"Oh, come on. I'm a middle-aged woman, okay? I'm not imagining this stuff," I protest, my tone pleading for him to drop it.

"Mary," he says gently, "I didn't see you as anything but beautiful, delicious, and fuckable. Still, you're right. Your body is yours to do with what you want."

His eyes glint again, and I watch his wheels turning as they graze over my body. "You know, when I was out in the garage, I saw the kinds of things you like to do with your body. When you're alone."

Well, fucking fuck with a fuck on top. I wanted to believe he didn't see me masturbate earlier, but the jig is up. I feel weirdly embarrassed that he saw that, even though we just boinked the living daylights out of each other ten minutes ago.

"Oh, did you?" I reply, playing it as cool as possible for someone with very little chill.

"I did. I'd like to see more of what you like to do to yourself, little toy," he purrs. "This one is new to me, too," he drawls, picking up the thrusting rabbit from the bed. "I wonder if you'd follow directions for Santa now. You were so nice for me earlier. Is your naughty side ready to come out?" he asks, walking toward me. "What do you think? Will you use this on yourself for me?"

My insecurity fades into static as it's replaced by the steady drumming of lust. This feels a lot more like that fantasy I wanted.

"Yes, Santa," I reply submissively.

"Mm," he purrs, nodding his head. "Good girl. Lay on the bed for Santa. I want to see what my toy can do."

I follow his directions, propping my pillows against the headboard and lying against them, then disobey, draping the quilt over my body. Then, I pick up the rabbit and look back up at him.

"What do I do now?"

"You're going to touch yourself. I want to see how my toy plays with herself when she's alone."

Fuck. My clit throbs.

I give him a playfully obstinate look, interested in how he'll react to me covering up what he asked to see. Swirling my wetness with my fingers under the quilt, I work some of it over the shaft of the rabbit vibrator, then stare right at him as I push the toy inside of me, wanting him to see the way my eyelids flutter and my mouth opens involuntarily as I do it. He lifts the corner of the quilt and pauses, his eyebrow raised impishly.

I drop the act. Everything about this evening is out of character, including how much I want him to watch me play with myself. When I don't tell him to stop, he whips the quilt off with a lecherous smile, immediately zeroing in on the toy in my pussy.

"Hey. You too," I reply, nodding my head toward his cock because my hands are occupied. "I want to watch you fuck your hand while I fuck myself with this rabbit."

Who am I right now?

Samson looks at me like he's fighting his instincts to control the situation. I see it in his eyes when he decides to drop it and settles next to me on top of the covers.

"Spit," he commands, holding out his palm. The surprising request jolts through me, amping me up. He could spit in his own hand or use the lube I put on the bedside table earlier, but he's going to make me do it. I like how he doesn't tiptoe around me. It's exhausting to be treated like fragile glass. I want this, for him to use me like his personal sex toy. Looking Samson straight in the eyes, I adjust the vibrator, lining the nub up perfectly against my clit, and spit into his palm. He never breaks his stare as he brings his hand to his cock, smearing my spit over his length.

"There's my good girl," he growls, and I quickly turn up the vibrator, hoping to play off my moan over his words as a moan for the toy. "I knew a good girl lived here."

I sink back against the pillow as I press the button to start the thrusting mechanism. The toy isn't extremely loud, but in this quiet room all you can hear is the *thump, thump, thump* of the toy inside me, until another rhythm matches it. There's no way to disguise the moan that comes out of me when I realize what he's doing. My jaw falls open as I watch Samson's hand match the rhythm of the toy, moving in time with the thrusting thumps inside me.

Taking deep breaths, I settle into the sensations, trying to distract myself from the erotic motion of his hand and the memory of how he felt doing that inside of me.

Samson nods his head at me. "Turn it up higher."

I mewl involuntarily, my arousal skyrocketing from the command. The vibrator is intense at this level, and my breath grows heavier, my pussy increasingly wet and swollen. Samson's strokes maintain the same thumping rhythm, but his grip and thrusts have grown in intensity as well. My focus moves from his hands on his cock up to his face, and he follows me, trailing his gaze up my body from my pussy to my mouth.

"Turn it up again," he commands, and I curse, reveling in how filthy the order feels with his intense eye contact. I press the button again.

Samson grips his cock harder. As I watch him work himself up and down, swirling his fingers through his pre-come to lubricate his movements, my moans take on a strained, erratic beat as they grow higher and higher.

"Yes, yes..." I scream out, impassioned cries coursing past my lips, building myself up to what promises to be an earth-shattering release.

Samson's hand moves wildly up and down his shaft, his grip tight around his wide length.

"Is my little toy getting close for Santa?"

I bite my lip, nodding my head yes with my chin tilted down and eyes angled up at him.

"*Fuck*, Mary. So good. You're doing so good. Come for me. Scream my name. I don't give a shit what's in that little pussy, I want my name on your lips."

"Fuuuuck, Samson," I cry out, repeating his name over and over with each pulse of my orgasm.

Just as I remove the toy from my pussy, Samson gets up on his knees next to me, his breath shallow as his fist pumps rapidly.

"Do you see what you do to me, little toy? Do I look like a man who doesn't like what he sees?" I watch his abs contract and his biceps flex with the frenzied movements of his hand. My desire becomes a fierce, brutal storm that sweeps me up as Samson reaches for the toy I just used and brings it to his mouth. Maintaining eye contact, he licks it from base to tip, tasting my release. His head falls back with a satisfied groan.

"Do you have any idea how fucking good you taste? How delicious your dripping pussy looks?"

I reach toward his length, but he shakes his head.

"It's my turn to tell you what *I* see when I look at you."

His hand moves faster, gripping his cock harder as he gazes at my naked body.

"I see your tits bouncing as you work that toy into your pretty pussy. Your eyelids creasing as you scream with pleasure. Your stretch marks shimmering on your hips as you grind against that toy. Your thighs quivering as you fall apart. I see all of it, Mary, and it's fucking beautiful."

Samson grunts out his last word, and then he's coming. He stares at my body as he comes undone, his release landing on my breasts, my stomach, my hips, my thighs, painting every spot I'd mentioned, every flaw. It makes me feel wildly powerful, sexy in a way I've never felt before.

When he's finished, he admires all the places he's covered me. With his finger, he swirls his come around my nipple, making it harden again. He pinches it, playing my body to perfection, and I moan. Staring at my lips, he soaks in the sounds as his fingers trail down my body.

"Fucking gorgeous. You gorgeous, gorgeous girl."

I blink in shock, like a record that's skipped on repeat, as I hear his words again and again. But it's not him saying them, now. My heart beats rapidly, all the air rushing out of my lungs in one fell swoop. Feeling my palms sweat, I become desperate for space as I quickly scurry out of the bed. Samson watches in confusion as I pace the floor, my breath tight in my chest.

CHAPTER 8

Will stands in front of me in a handsome navy blue suit, wearing what I call his 'little boy smile'. His lips spread as far across his face as they can reach, and a little peek of his tongue slips out from the left side of his straight, white teeth. It's somehow a smile that both looks like Christmas morning and like he's planning the most mischievous deeds; angelic until you see that slip of tongue, making you question things. He squeezes my hands twice, barely listening to the man in front of us as he speaks his line and then pauses for Will to take his turn.

"Mary, as the facts and figures guy in this relationship, I am well aware that making lifelong promises at age 26 is somewhat like looking at my dad's ear hair and denying that will be me in 30 years. (Sorry, Dad.) But what I'm trying to say is that I'm going to change, and you're going to change, too. You might start taking out the trash, and I might start remembering to grab the mail on the way in the house. I mean, truly anything is possible, I suppose.

"So, what I'm promising you is that I will always take care of you. I'll always support you. I'll always buy another bookcase when you run out of space or set up another shelf in the garage when you get tired of another hobby. There's a whole multiverse of potential future Mary's and whichever ones I get, I'll be the luckiest Will in the world. I'm not scared of the future, any future, as long as I'm living it with you. The only change I couldn't *handle would be not having you by my side. I am yours, all of yours, every single Mary, forever, but especially the one standing in front of me right now. My gorgeous, gorgeous girl."*

"Mary, what's wrong? What happened?" Samson whispers sweetly.

I don't speak as I pace the room, mostly because breathing still feels difficult, but also because I have no clue what to say. The longer my silent pacing goes on, the more of an explanation I'll need, though. I try to get my heart to stop pounding before I speak.

"I'm going to get a drink," I announce to the room, avoiding eye contact with Samson as I grab an oversized t-shirt and stop in the bathroom to clean myself off before going to the kitchen.

Staring into the fridge, I try to determine the strongest drink I could make that wouldn't be a dead giveaway that a fairly normal combination of words triggered me this badly.

God. Is this how it's always going to be? I'll be lying in the afterglow and some man will say 'calzones' and I'll have a fucking panic attack because that was Will and I's Sunday dinner tradition?

The seconds tick by as I hear Samson moving around in the bedroom, knowing he's going to come out here.

I should probably just tell him, but it feels so good to be handled this way, rough and dominant, like I'm sturdy enough to take it. He might treat me differently once he learns I'm a widow. I can't undo that. I can't wipe his memory clean and start over. Once the widow cat is out of the bag, there's no putting it back in.

I hear Samson's footsteps as he approaches. He presses his chest against my back, rubbing my shoulders. I can tell it's well meaning, but the closeness of our bodies sets off my panic again, and I roll my shoulders to get his hands off me.

"Mary, I'm so sorry. Was it the way I came on you? Fuck." The air is cooler, easier to breathe, once he takes a few steps away.

"No," I say softly, just above a whisper. "It wasn't any of that." Suddenly, the idea of him touching me, protecting me, sounds like exactly what I want. "You can come back."

Samson's large hand spreads out on my back, rubbing me gently but not caging me in. It helps. I'm not scared of him or upset at him. What I fear is my reaction. I knew it was taking me a long time to act on my loneliness, over two years, but I thought I'd be fine once I did. It takes the wind out of my sails to realize how strong the grip of the past remains.

"Do you want me to make you a drink?" he asks softly.

I nod, heading to the table to sit.

"Fuck," Samson swore roughly. "I'm so fucking sorry. I know what it feels like to have something set you off like that."

After two years of this, I do too, though I wish I didn't.

"Oh, eggnog. You want a glass?" he asks, swiveling his head toward me.

I bark out a loud, surprised laugh. "Don't you think I'm already upset enough?"

He turns to me, his expression furrowed in confusion. "What do you mean? It's the only open alcohol in your fridge."

"You look pretty buff, so maybe drinking eggs seems normal to you, but it's not my thing. I haven't had it in a long time, so I bought some, but I have officially learned my lesson. Anyway, I think I'm good. I'm gonna go lie down again."

Samson shuts the fridge and follows me into the bedroom, moving two pillows against the headboard so I can rest against them. He gently covers my body with the quilt, and the warm, caring way he treats me triggers the release of a few heavy tears. I didn't even realize I'd been shivering until the quilt glides over my legs.

"I'll be right back."

When he re-enters the room, he hands me a glass of water. I move to set it on the nightstand, but Samson gently guides my hand and the glass back to my lap.

"Please drink it. We've had an intense night, and that can do a number on your body if you don't address it."

I sip the water, staring off into space, my body limp except for my grip on the glass as Samson gently strokes my leg over the quilt. He demands nothing, just sits through this with me. After feeling alone for so long, having someone to lie next to makes me feel steadier. My breathing slowly returns closer and closer to normal until the glass is empty and I set it down.

"Gorgeous," I sigh.

"What was that?" Samson replies, leaning closer to me. He rubs my arm as he waits patiently for my response.

"Gorgeous, gorgeous, girl," I repeat.

"That was the thing?"

"Yeah, I know that's ridiculous," I reply, my finger tracing the stitches of the quilt.

He extends his palm to cradle my cheek, gently guiding me to look at him.

"It's not, okay? You feeling comfortable and safe is not ridiculous. It's the most important thing."

"Thanks," I reply.

"What about what we did physically? Was that too much, and then the phrase set you off?"

I pause for a moment, considering.

"No, I liked it. I liked the way you, uh, came on me," I reply, trying to be open, at least about the sex we had. "It felt hot the whole time. I was fine until the end."

Samson continues to rub my arm reassuringly. "He really did a number on you, huh?"

You don't know the half of it.

I decide at that moment that Samson has enough information to understand. He's clearly a caring person, despite the rough exterior. I don't want him walking on glass around me, because I like the dynamic between us. He's Santa, and I'm his toy. He doesn't need to know how broken I am.

"Yeah, I'm used to it."

"Maybe you're used to it, but you deserve to feel safe, Mary. Cared for."

It's not that no one cared about me, it's that someone *did*, and then he was ripped away from me.

"You're probably right."

"Maybe we could have a safe word. If things get too intense, or too triggering, you could stop everything with one word."

"I didn't really know until it was too late, though."

"That's the perfect time to use a safe word, so I know to stop immediately."

I can't tell if he means next time with *us*, or in general. This night was fun, which is something I haven't allowed myself enough of lately.

"Maybe 'Santa'," I joke with a small smile.

"A safe word needs to be something you're not likely to say otherwise," Samson answers with a wink.

"Hmm. Jingle bells," I respond.

He pinches my side playfully, and I yelp.

"That's fine," Samson laughs, "but safe words really are important."

Releasing a sigh, I lean my body against his, and he wraps his arm around me. The physical touch after so long without it makes me feel emotional, but I try not to let Samson in on how significant it is to me.

"Is it okay if I stay here?" Samson gestures to the bed.

Yet again, I love the way he asks for my consent, even over something as small as where to sleep. There's only one bed, anyway, so the only other place he could sleep is the couch, which would be far too small for his frame.

"Stay," I answer. He's been inside me, there's no reason he can't sleep next to me. It feels intimate, but I brush the feeling aside. It's practical, nothing more.

Readjusting the pillows, I sink down into the bed and get comfortable. Samson joins me under the covers, and then I feel large, warm fingers trailing up and down my belly. I sigh into the sensation, looking up at him.

"You're pretty great at taking care of people when they're upset, you know."

His face falls, sadness washing over his expression for just a moment, and then he gives me a tight smile.

"What did I say wrong?" I ask.

"I've had a lot more practice dealing with tough shit than I'd like," he responds with a sigh, letting his head fall against the pillow and staring at the ceiling.

"Like what?" I want to know what images he's seeing play out as he stares up there, but quickly realize that's way too personal, especially since I'm keeping secrets too. His eyes shut.

"Hey, I'm sorry," I whisper. "You don't have to answer that."

He turns to me, stroking up and down my belly with lazy fingers. "I liked taking care of you tonight." His lips form a small smile as he watches his fingers move on my stomach.

"Well, I meant it. You're fantastic at it. It felt… nice."

As he continues dancing his fingers over my stomach and thighs, my eyes close, focused only on the feeling of his hands on my skin.

When Samson leaves, I'll have to thank him for making me realize that life has good surprises as well as bad ones. My languid, content sigh is the last sound I hear before the night goes silent and sleep overtakes me.

CHAPTER 9

Sunlight streams through the window as I wake. Blinking my eyes open, I expect to see the normal city view from my condo, glass and metal skyscrapers juxtaposed with shorter, mural covered brick buildings. Instead, I'm staring at rounded log walls framing a small window with plaid curtains. The view through the window is pure white, interrupted by slivers of green fir trees enshrouded by the night's snow. I'm expecting a mess of clothes and sex toys strewn about when I get out of bed, but the space is clean. My clothes are folded in the laundry basket I packed them in, and my toys sit in a tidy line on my dresser, minus the rabbit toy from last night.

Dragging myself out of bed, I head to the bathroom on leaden legs. After I splash water on my face to wake up, I notice the clean rabbit toy sitting on the ledge of the sink. My heart rate increases as I brush my teeth, trying to control my panic.

Samson isn't here.

Every trace of our night together has been tidied up and put away. Sure, I wasn't expecting any sort of future with the biker Santa Claus sex god, but I thought I had a bit more time. I assumed I'd at least be able to say goodbye after sleeping with someone new for the first time in two years.

Making my way to the kitchen, I automatically release a pleased sigh as I smell the fresh coffee in the coffeemaker's carafe. The coffeemaker looks so clean I can see it shining from several feet away, a distinct change from last night. How tired was I, that I didn't hear any of this? The thoughtfulness of him making me coffee before he left makes my chest pang. My fist clenches, and I slam it on the counter.

Damn it.

I'm not naïve enough to get emotionally tangled up in what was apparently a one-night stand, but some part of me hoped the one-night stand would include a bit of the morning. I mean, how'd he even get out of here with that wonky bike? Did the roads clear that quickly? It pains me to admit, but I kind of fantasized about waking up in his arms.

Instead, I woke up in a drafty cabin, alone, per usual. "I'm used to it," I told Samson last night. The admission sounded sad yesterday evening, but alone in the morning light, I decide to take comfort in it. I've been surviving just fine like this. I'm comfortable alone.

Trying to remember my original plan for this weekend, (before I allowed myself to be Santa's little ho ho ho for the night), I pour a cup of coffee and add the peppermint mocha creamer I impulse bought for this trip. Sitting at the dining table, I give in, allowing myself a mini pity party, but only for the duration of this cup of coffee. Right as the first sip hits my lips, a loud thud reverberates from the back of the cabin, startling me. The coffee mug jerks in my hand, splashing all over my robe and naked chest.

"Fuckity fucking fuck balls," I curse. The robe is already a lost cause, so I use it to wipe the rest of the coffee off my chest and the table.

Flinging the soiled robe into the corner of the bedroom, I root through the laundry basket for underwear and fresh clothes. Hurriedly, I pull on a pair of fleece leggings and an oversized fair isle sweater that says 'Challah at Your Girl' with a big loaf of bread underneath. The fair isle pattern has menorah, dreidel, and Jewish star details. Will was Jewish, so we'd developed a lot of Chrismukkah traditions, including exchanging silly sweaters to wear to holiday parties.

I slip on my boots and take a few last gulps of the coffee before plopping it back on the table and heading out the door to investigate the noise. As I walk around back, I'm glad to see that the storm has passed. The cold air doesn't have the bite it had last night, and the sun feels warm on my skin. Heavy plinks of melted snow drip off the roof as I crunch through the gravel.

Whatever I expected to find, it wasn't the scene in front of me as I round the corner to the back of the cabin. I pause, leaning against the house, trying not to interrupt Samson so I can watch him. For a fantasy fling, it bothers me how much I cared he was gone, and it bugs me even more how relieved I am to find him back here. All of that quickly fades to background noise, drowned out by the sexiest thing I've seen in a long time.

Samson grunts loudly as he hoists a round log of wood onto a big stump. Once he drops it in place, he pants, assessing the piece of wood in front of him. He smooths his hand over the top of the log and slaps it, caressing the face of the wood, feeling it run along his fingers.

Immediately my mind is in the gutter. 'Age-Gap Biker Santa' is already a pretty freaking niche kink, so I really don't need to add a lumberjack fetish, but here we are. Watching his muscles flex as he manhandles obscenely large pieces of wood with a strained grunt, I'm catapulted into yet another erotic fantasy.

The same way he hoists the log onto the stump, I picture him lifting me by my thighs, his hands moving to my ass as his tongue delves inside my mouth in a determined kiss. How he'd slap me on the ass before throwing me down on the bed, my body splayed out for him to do whatever he sees fit.

Samson is wearing a plaid button-up I don't recognize over his jeans and boots from last night. He must have found it somewhere in the cabin. After my little episode last night, I'm relieved that I don't have any emotional reaction to the shirt. My body, on the other hand, responds strongly as the fabric strains over his muscles when he picks up an ax. He grips it in his large, powerful hand as he huffs, preparing himself to chop into the round, uncut piece of hardwood.

In my fantasy, he stands at the side of the bed, staring down at me laid out for him. He unbuttons his shirt, his abs flexing as he strips out of his jeans and boots. Gripping his thick, veiny cock in his hand, he strokes himself until he's hard, staring down at my body intensely.

"Let's fuckin' go," Samson growls, looking down at the round of wood, looking down at my body.

He lifts the ax above his head, his arms tense, focused on the center of the log. The ax lands in the middle like a bullseye, cutting about a third of the way through the wood.

"So goddamn juicy," he groans.

Samson backs away from the log, wiping his brow, and walks a shallow circle around it. Approaching it again, Samson examines the split, using his hands to investigate his work so far. His breath comes in shallow pants.

My hand reaches into my panties involuntarily now, needing to do something about the ache in my core. I imagine myself splaying my legs wide open, totally on display. I moan at the idea, and real-life Samson looks up at me, a lewd smile spreading over his face as he sees where my hand has gone.

"This is a beautiful split, I'm gonna get some good work done here," he says with a wink.

He strikes the wood again and deepens the cut. It wobbles from the force, moving away from the center of the stump. He grunts as he moves it back in place.

My mind swirls, imagining Samson's fingers on my overstimulated clit, how I'd squirm, trying to back away from him as he worked my body, but he wouldn't let me. He'd follow me forward instead, shifting to lie on his stomach. Pressing his palm into my lower belly to steady me as his tongue joined his hands, he'd explore every inch between my thighs.

"Stay there. Stay right fucking there."

He fixes his grip on the ax, his forearms bulging as he finds the right hold on the sharp tool. I begin saying something, but he shakes his head, refocusing his gaze on the wood in front of him. I swirl figure eights on my clit mercilessly, working myself up, closing in on my release.

"C'mon, let's finish this."

He swings again and again, his arms bringing the blade down on the thick, hard wood repeatedly. Each swing widens the gap in the wood more and more until his last swing breaks the giant log in half. He tosses the ax to the side with a curse, lifting his plaid shirt to wipe the sweat from his brow, giving me a tantalizing view of his flexed abs. He breathes heavily as he looks at the two halves of wood he split.

I'm so close to climax, I'm lost between what's real and not. In my fantasy, my moans shift into screams as I beg him to keep going, to not stop, to stay right there. I might be screaming in real life, I honestly don't know or care anymore, and then I come undone, my thighs quaking as the orgasm takes over.

Samson walks right up to me, breathing heavily as he guides me up against the wall. He traces his finger up from my panting chest to underneath my chin, lifting my face to look at him.

"That feel good, little toy?"

Yes.

I nod. My breathing is heavy as I stare up into his deep blue eyes, watching his pupils dilate as he stares into my post-orgasm face. I remember how I felt waking up, when I thought he was gone, then how I felt as soon as I saw him, how quickly I lost myself to the fantasy of his body on mine. I've been worried about my intense reaction to him, but I didn't recognize it for what it was- lust. Lust isn't that scary. There's nothing wrong with giving in to this fantasy, this lust. Samson is simply a body I can use to release this dam of sexual need that's been building within me.

"You gonna come inside with me?" he says with a smirk, and my body and brain both answer *yes.*

CHAPTER 10

Samson is sweaty with exertion as he holds my hand, walking us straight to the shower. He pulls my sweatshirt and leggings off while we wait for it to heat, and then step in together. We take turns washing our hair and bodies, but the proximity of his naked form to mine proves too much after the intense orgasm I just had, and I need to touch him. I run my wet, soapy hand up and down his shaft until he's thrusting back at me with every stroke. He turns me around, my chest hitting the tile with a wet smack, and places his cock between my thighs.

"Thank god," I moan, arching for him, but he lands a painful, wet smack against my ass.

"Not yet, little toy. I'm going to use you all day, however I want."

All day?

The question floats away as his length slides between my thighs, spreading my slit around his thick shaft. His cock stimulates my clit with each pass of his head against my sensitive flesh. He rasps out a deep, gravelly groan, and I whine in needy frustration as he continues moving back and forth along me, but not in me. I try to arch, notching him in place, but he gives me another playful slap on the ass as he repositions himself horizontal along my center.

"I don't have a condom right now," he says as he continues gliding along my sensitive flesh.

"I have an IUD," I whisper nervously. "So, I don't mind if you don't use..."

Samson nips at my ear from behind. "Good to know. Now be quiet and let me play how I want, little toy."

He hooks two fingers into the side of my mouth as he picks up speed, then grips my hips as he slides his cock along me over and over. I press my thighs together, enjoying the way he glides along my sensitive nerves, even though I'm desperate for more. My clit swells with the tempo of his thrusts, the wet slap of his pelvis against my ass sounding out like a drum as my keening moans grow louder and louder, filling the small bathroom.

"That's right, sing for me. Loud, like a fucking Christmas caroler. Sing for me, little toy. Scream."

Samson's filthy commands have me wailing, shattered cries streaming out like water as I push back into him with each of his thrusts and my orgasm rockets through me. My clit throbs against his length as his release sprays all over the green-tiled wall. Afterward, he drags my back against his chest, cradling me as he runs his hands along my wet curves. We hold each other, our bodies pressed together as we both come back down to earth.

Watching the water rinse his cum off the wall, I tell him, "This has been a much whiter Christmas than I expected."

"Mm," Samson responds, gliding his hands over my body. "Are you talking about the snowstorm, or the sex?"

"Yes," I respond, nodding. He wraps his arms even tighter around me, kissing the top of my head. The kiss sparks a wave of concern that this is getting too intimate, so I back away, stepping out of the shower to dry off.

I need a minute away from the intensity that is Samson, so I head to the bedroom to get dressed, but I end up sitting on top of the wooden chest instead, trying to gather my thoughts. I've never reacted like this to anyone, this visceral arousal that overtakes me when he's around.

A minute later, I feel a prickle of awareness at my back and turn, knowing what I'll find. Well, almost. I expected Samson in a towel, but I find him leaning against the doorway, totally naked.

"Did you think we were done?" he asks, his left brow raised.

"I haven't been doing a lot of thinking since you arrived, Samson. Are you planning on staying?"

"I'm going with the flow, Mary. Why, you need a detailed itinerary? I'd email you one, but I'm sure there's no Wi-Fi out here."

I fling a pillow at him, and he catches it, throwing it right back at me.

"I've been watching your wheels whirl around in there ever since I showed up. You wanna tell me about it?"

Part of me does. After the delicate, caring way he treated me last night, I know it would be safe to tell him, but it also worries me that the caring, comforting side of him would kick in too much, and that's not what I want from him right now. I want the animal, the dominant, this dirty side of him.

"I really don't. Thanks, though." He gives me a look that says I'm in trouble. "How about I tell you what I want next?" I purr.

I spin around on the wooden chest, crawling up onto the bed with my hips swaying seductively, then lie down on my back facing him. Pulling my knees up so my feet are flat on the bed, I spread them apart, using my fingers to splay my pussy open for him.

"Play with your little toy. Please."

"Naughty, greedy little thing, you are," Samson groans as he immediately moves between my thighs. His pupils dilate as he stares down at me, spread open for him. Catching him off guard, I grab him by the hips and twist him down so his back is on the bed while I rise to my knees.

"I am greedy," I tell him, my fingers brushing down along his abs to reach his length, then taking him in my hands and stroking firmly. He hisses through his teeth as his cock hardens in my grip. My brain goes quiet, content, as I bend over his body, swirling my tongue around his nipple. A wave of power comes over me when my playful bite causes his cock to twitch.

"But I won't make any extra work for Santa, I promise. What I have next on my list is a job just for me."

My tongue traces the line of hair down his abs, and a heady lust comes over me as I grip his powerful thigh to steady myself. His hard cock taps just below my chin, leaving a smear of pre-come along my throat. Remembering the expert way he took my body over the edge, I desperately need my turn at that kind of power, need to affect him even half as much as he's affecting me. By the time I rise from my knees, I'll have had him roaring as I taste his salty cum on my tongue.

My hands remain on Samson's thigh, using only my tongue to tease his cock, tracing his length down all the way to the base, alternating light kisses with gentle licks until I feel him throbbing against me. My lips glide over his head as if I'm going to take him in my mouth, but I back off at the last second to continue lightly licking and kissing him. Releasing my hands from his thighs, I immediately begin stroking up and down his shaft while I torture his head with my tongue. He growls with need as his hips move in a gentle thrusting movement, begging me to take him in my mouth.

Oral sex has always been something that gives me a feeling of power and control, and it radiates through me in this moment. Kneeling beside him in this submissive position, I relish the way his desire is reliant on my tongue, my mouth, my hands. His entire cock is about to slide between my teeth, requiring his submission as much as mine. This powerful, muscular man lies next to me, and I know *I'm* going to be the one to make him come undone.

Finally, I watch his expression as I lower my lips down his length, how his jaw tenses and nostrils flare. The feeling of his cock stretching my lips makes me moan, and the vibrations make his cock jerk again. As he hits the back of my throat, I gag, pulling up and then sinking all the way down his length again. I remind myself to relax my throat and then swallow, savoring the feeling of him sliding past my larynx into my throat. I love this feeling, and the euphoria of the moment makes me want to go further and test my limits.

I'm playing with fire, but as long as I hold the match, I'm in control.

Samson groans harshly, moving his hands to the back of my head to take control. I shake my head no, using my hands to remove his, placing them back on the bed. They curl into fists as I hollow my cheeks, increasing my suction on his cock while simultaneously picking up speed.

A person can only produce so much saliva, and my mouth is getting dry as it sucks up and down his shaft. Popping off his cock with an audible sound, I look into his eyes and open my mouth. His brows furrow. He's getting close, but not close enough yet to come in my mouth.

"Spit."

The corner of his mouth curls in a filthy smile, hopefully remembering how he asked me to spit for him yesterday as he returns the favor, bending over lasciviously and spitting into my mouth.

"Thank you, Santa. One more, please."

He spits again, then lifts off the bed to a standing position, dragging me down to my knees on the floor, his eyes dark as coal as they gaze into mine. We're engaged in a silent battle for control now, but he doesn't seem to recognize how stubborn I am when I decide something. Sinking my finger into my mouth, I coat it in our joined spit. My other hand grips his length, bobbing my head vigorously on his shaft. His breathing picks up speed, and I know he's getting close to finishing.

It might be a week before Christmas, but I'm determined to set off New Year's fireworks.

As I work his length with my hand and mouth, my other hand reaches behind him. My finger is still wet with his spit as I circle his rim, coating it before I press my finger into his ass up to the first knuckle. He gasps, his cock twitching again as I slowly work my finger in further, locating his prostate and massaging it. His hips lose their rhythm, but my mouth moves with them, pulling him deep into me as he curses and grunts. My finger keeps massaging inside him as he grips the back of my head again. I'm doing so many things at once that this time, I let him hold me. He sighs in relief as he shoves his entire cock into my mouth, filling me up to my throat. I swallow around him again as he growls heavily, releasing spurts of cum down my throat, my finger milking his prostate until he pulls his softening cock out of my mouth.

Samson's hands release their grip on my hair, stroking over the brunette strands as he gazes into my eyes with that stare of his, dark as the night but bright like stars.

"Good girl," he praises, "my naughty, filthy, good girl."

"Mm," I respond, leaning forward, vibrating against his cock as I lick him clean. A powerful energy buzzes through me, and I don't mind if he says 'my good girl' as if I'm his. If I am, I'm a rental, and I set all the terms.

"You still want more?" he asks, petting my damp hair, pushing it away from my face. I lick up the entire underside of his cock from the base up, pressing my tongue into the sensitive slit of his head and then sit back, nodding obediently.

"Let's play, little toy. Let's make a fucking mess."

"God. Fuck. Yes."

———

Time loses meaning as our bodies explore each other. However long it's been, it's simultaneously not enough and too much. My hips hover over Samson in a squat as I move myself up and down his length. The angle is just right, his cock perfectly stroking deep within me.

"Use me. Get that little pussy off with my cock."

I whine in response, my body sore and overstimulated but still begging for more. We've spent the morning in so many positions it'd make a porn director blush. Leaning forward, I place my hands on his hard chest to steady my tired body. The angle pushes my clit into his pelvis as I move in slow circles on top of him, rolling against his body exactly the way I need it. I feel like an animal, driven by my basest instincts, growing wild with my inability to finish. My eyes are pleading as I look into Samson's, begging him to take over, to help me come.

"I've got you, little toy. Santa will give you what you need."

He picks me up like a rag doll as he scoots out from underneath me. My legs hang off the side of the bed as he places me face down on it. I hear his footsteps as he walks to the dresser, and when he returns, I hear a click and a buzzing noise begin. Lifting my hips like they're nothing, Samson places a bullet vibrator underneath me, directly on my clit. A surprised squeak leaves my lips as my entire body trembles from the intensity of the vibration. He nudges my feet together until my thighs touch, trapping the toy, and then he works his thick length through my closed thighs and into my pussy. Each heavy thrust grinds the vibrator onto my sore clit, and I shout obscenities as he ravages my body.

"Fuck, Samson. That's it."

My hands reach over my head, gripping the quilt as he slams mercilessly against my deepest walls.

"I see you, little toy," he grunts, his tempo increasing. "I know exactly what to do with you."

Snaking my hand underneath me, I clasp the vibrator tighter against my clit until I'm choking out a scream. My pussy clenches so hard against his cock that Samson sounds pained as he roars out his orgasm right after me. After a few moments, he withdraws, grasping my waist in his powerful hands and tossing my spent body onto the bed. He flips my exhausted limbs over until I'm on my back, and my legs flop open. I can feel how much of a mess I am, with my knotted, sweaty hair and raw, drenched pussy.

Samson caresses my core, smearing our joined release over my swollen flesh. "You don't know what it does to me, seeing you like this. This is something... different, Mary. Can you feel it? I don't just want to use you, I need to. I need to devour you."

If I felt like an animal before, he sounds like one now. He yanks my thighs open further with a feral intensity, then turns the vibrator off, flinging it across the bed with a beastly grunt.

"Fuck," he curses, walking out of the room.

I lie there, sated and content, but confused. I don't know where he's gone or why, but when I hear the front door open, I lift my head in question. He has a palmful of snow in his hand, and he's lasered in on my pussy as he walks back into the room, cupping the snow into a ball. The next second he's surging toward me, pressing the snowball against my spread pussy. A shrieking curse echoes through the room as I lurch up, the cold snow shocking my exhausted body.

Samson crashes to his knees, wrapping his arms under my thighs to slide my hips to the end of the bed. My brain attempts to process all the conflicting sensations- the dripping wetness, the burning cold, and the rawness of my pussy, simultaneously soothed and pained by the ball of snow between my thighs.

"I haven't had a snow cone in a long time. This might be the best one I'll ever have."

Samson's face settles between my thighs as his tongue laps at the snow. The swiping of his tongue forces the snow deeper inside me, and I lose all rational thought as his warm tongue alternates with the cold snow. Samson devours the melting, messy, snow cone he's turned my pussy into, and my soreness dissipates into a cool, slightly numb sensation.

He continues licking and tasting me until the snow is gone and my eyes finally relax closed. It's only the early afternoon, but he lets me rest as he towels me off and then shifts my head to the pillow, tucking me under the quilt. Gently caressing my hair, Samson hums what sounds like a Christmas song, the deep tone lulling me to sleep as reality fades to black.

CHAPTER 11

wake with a start, having a very Robin Williams in Jumanji "What year is it?!" moment. Turning to roll over, I smack my head into something hard. When the object laughs his familiar, bold 'huh, huh, huh', I fall back onto my pillow with an "umph", rubbing the sleep out of my eyes.

"Ow," I mumble to myself, "Were you asleep or were you watching me like a creep?"

"Are those my only two options?"

"Preparing yourself to fuck me in my sleep, maybe?" I joke.

"Why would your mind go to *that*, of all things? Maybe you're the creep," he laughs.

"I've read a lot of smutty books, you never know."

"Not my thing, little toy. I wouldn't be fucking you properly if you could sleep through it." He regards me thoughtfully. "What if I *was* watching you, but not in a creepy way?"

I consider that. It feels like too intense of a thing for a weekend fling. Still, I'm strangely drawn to Samson, and I want a little more information about the man attached to the cock I'm enjoying so much.

"So, what do you do with your weekend when you're not seducing lonely women in remote cabins?" I ask him as I sit upright against the headboard.

He gives me a flinty look. "You're assuming, little toy. You think this is a regular occurrence for me?"

"Uh, yes. Of course, I do."

"Why?"

I give him a look. He's playing dumb.

"Come on. Don't give me that. Because of the way your freaking face looks, Samson. Have you seen your body? And your filthy mouth, and the way you use your fingers and your cock. This isn't your first rodeo, and I'm not the first horse you've ridden into oblivion."

"Mm," he responds, his head tilting again, as if he's trying to figure me out. "I've never given a woman so many orgasms and have her try to act like it's nothing to her."

My head whips toward him, taking in his impish grin. "Who says I'm doing that?"

"Come on, don't give me that," he mimics. "Your walls are more secure than a penitentiary."

"Maybe that's on purpose, to keep out things I don't want," I lie. Any walls I have are shoddy and haphazard at best, crumbling under the intensity of his gaze.

"No. You like this, Mary, I can tell. I think your ex really messed you up, but you crave this little cat-and-mouse thing. And it's all good, because I fucking love it, too."

"You think you've got such a good read on me after a single day. I know you're confident, Samson, but you don't know everything."

"Oh, but I do know that, little toy. I know you're hiding a lot behind all that barbed wire. Why don't you tell me, then?"

"Because you don't need to know. This is just a weekend thing, nothing more. I needed a nice cock, and ideally a good mouth and fingers, and you're supplying that. Don't pretend like this is some Hallmark Christmas movie when it's clearly slutty Santa porn."

Samson's eyes gleam as he sits up, his muscles tense like a predator ready to pounce. I've let my frustration stream out, and instead of taking it badly, it almost looks like it turns him on.

Shit. This can't be good, but it's sexy as fuck.

"My little mouse wants to play, does she? You want to push me away? Want to run? Fine. Run. I'll catch you."

God, the way he takes my emotions and spins them into a sexual game is so fucking hot. My chest rises and falls in heavy breaths, considering all my options. Only one dominates my thoughts, sending shockwaves of heat through my body. Stepping out of bed, I keep Samson in view as I head to my laundry basket and start grabbing clothes. I throw on leggings, thick wool socks, a sports bra and his discarded flannel shirt from this morning.

There's something in his eyes, in the deep, slow breaths he takes, his tense, coiled muscles, that tells me I've awoken something primal in Samson. He's still naked, making no movements, but his eyes are alert. My adrenaline skyrockets. He beholds me like an apex predator, completely still in order not to startle me, while I respond similarly, trying not to trigger him into pouncing. I want the chase, the feeling of being alive, everything he's offering me right now.

Something niggles at me, telling me I might want it too much, and it's that thought that has me sprinting to the front door, stepping quickly into my boots and taking off toward the woods out back, slamming the front door behind me.

I really should have joined Will on some of those 5 am runs.

I kick myself for my love of sleeping in and general disdain for exercising as I sprint as fast as I can across the field behind the cabin. I need to make it through the tree line and into the woods before he sees me. My eyes scan the field leading to the woods. Once I get there I can hide, but out here I'm too exposed. My heartbeat skyrockets when I hear the front door slam shut, and I know that was Samson's warning.

My body erupts in shivers and arousal floods my core as I run as fast as I can. Although I'd never admit it to Samson, this *is* a fantasy of mine, one I've kept locked away deep in my brain because I'd never actually ask for it. If I asked Will to chase me through the streets of Chicago, he'd get arrested. Even if we found a way, we'd probably have ended up a silly, laughing mess instead of the wild, feral feeling coursing through me now.

Slush and mud splash up my legs, soaking into my leggings. As I stretch my legs as far as they can go, air rushing in and out of my lungs, I'm overcome by a sense of euphoria. My body and my mind are one, working together, pushing themselves. The endorphins give me a rush of energy and power. I feel wild, like a deer bounding away from a wolf.

This time, I didn't freeze in the face of my fears. No. I chose to fight.

As I hit the tree line I slink behind a large sturdy trunk, taking deep, hard breaths. Turning back toward the cabin, my body erupts into chills as I watch Samson jogging steadily toward me. His piercing eyes focus straight in on me.

I'm the deer, alright. Prey.

Endorphins and adrenaline swirl through me as I launch forward again, sprinting into the woods. I keep my eyes on the ground as I jump over fallen branches, crunching through the bed of leaves scattered on the forest floor. The melting snow makes things slick and wet, and my body thrums with awareness that one wrong move could end the hunt.

I spot an enormous, thick tree a few yards in front of me and swing myself behind it. My back hits the bark, my hot breath billowing white in front of me, as I listen to the forest. It's too quiet in the dead of winter, no bugs or birds to drown out the sound of my feet. Even small noises are deafeningly loud in this kind of silence. My blood freezes as I hear the chains of Samson's boots rattling over the fallen leaves, breaking twigs underneath the force of his heavy, solid body. A deep shiver rises through me, shaking my limbs and rattling my teeth.

I forget the point of it all in this moment, who we are, where we are, whether I wanted him to catch me or not. Survival instinct takes over, that animal part of my brain telling me to run, to resist.

Samson has stopped moving and the forest stills with him, eerily quiet as the late afternoon sun casts its shadows everywhere. I follow the sun's path with my eyes, noting how my shadow trails behind me, beyond the tree's protection. I can't stay here.

My body shoots out from the tree toward the cabin, hoping he's gone further into the woods already. My feet fly below me until they hit a knotty root hidden under the leaves, and then I'm tumbling in terror toward the ground.

Fuck. No. Get yourself the fuck up, Mary. We're not going to let something small like, I don't know, a complete lack of running experience and muscle tone stop us.

Scrambling to my feet, I feel the scrapes on my palms and the tear in my leggings but ignore them. My blood pumps rapidly as I run, focusing on the ground to avoid another fall. This is just a game, I tell myself.

In real life, the worst thing that could knock me down already did. As I dash through the woods, I consider if I ever got back up from that. Maybe I did, but only to continue fleeing from the past. Have I let myself race toward anything new? Am I going to spend the rest of my life skittering away from the past, or will I stop and set a fresh course?

All at once, I sense Samson's presence. My heart thumps so loud in my chest that it feels like he must be able to hear it. I spot his shadow on the ground just before I feel his arm extending in front of me, blocking my body and pulling me in. His arm knocks an "oof" out of my lungs as my back thuds against his chest and his hands wrap around my chest and throat.

"I can feel your heart, little toy. Is it beating this wildly for me?"

I attempt to wriggle out of his grip, testing how tightly he's holding me.

"Did you want to get caught? Is that why you ran straight back into my arms?"

My body reacts to his taunts with renewed determination as I stubbornly attempt to twist my body, flailing my legs. My animal instinct wants to get away even though my blood heats from having him so close. When my swinging leg slams into his shin, he grunts, the surprise blow causing his grip to slip the smallest amount, just enough for me to yank myself free.

I lurch forward, power gathering in my muscles to flee, but he lunges after me. His hand grabs my thigh, sending my momentum downward. Samson settles on his knees behind me, his body folding over mine and caging me in.

"I told you I would catch you, little toy," he growls triumphantly in my ear.

His hands grip the front of my flannel shirt beneath me and pull it apart in one swift tug, sending buttons flying out amongst the leaves. My tired body submits to his strength as I relax into the ground, craving the beast he's become in these woods.

My senses all focus in on his hard length as he traps me against the evidence of his need. I nuzzle my hips into him, grinding myself on his length until he grips my ponytail, yanking my body up against his with a savage grunt. His hands skate along the bare skin of my abdomen, up to my sports bra, my chest heaving against his palms. When his fingers hit my pebbled nipples he groans hoarsely, gripping my breast as his teeth bite at the base of my neck like an animal. I revel in the way my body affects him, the way the hunt has brought out this primal side of him.

"What happens next, little mouse? Tell me. Tell me what I'm going to do with my toy now that I've caught her."

"Take me," I pant heavily. "You caught me, so take me. Fuck me into the dirt."

He groans as his hand grasps my pussy through my leggings, his fingers stroking up and down my clit through the muddy fabric. The cold, damp feeling of the fabric against my heated core causes my body to curl in on itself with a quick gasp, his muscular arms the only thing holding me upright.

"That's right, Mary. You ran away, but I caught you, like we both fucking knew I would. Now beg for it. You wanted a beast, you got one. But I need to know you need this as much as I do."

"Please, fuck, I need you. Fuck me like an animal. I want it."

"As you wish," Samson snarls as he yanks my leggings down my legs, immobilizing me, trapped by the fabric bunched between my knees. He releases my hair, shoving me down onto my hands and knees. The only sound in the frozen forest is his zipper coming undone and then he's there, his cock hot against my entrance.

My head falls forward with relief, desperate for the reward, the punishment, whatever he's about to give. His cock glides along my slit, coating his head in the arousal gathering between my legs, and then he thrusts into me in one brutal push.

I howl underneath him, loving the feeling of being this full. Each forceful thrust puts pressure on my skinned knees and palms, but the pain centers me on the fierce, animal lust I'm feeling. Samson does what he promised, fucking me like a beast, his grip bruising my hips while his cock slams into me over and over.

Desire floods my brain as I arch my back and bellow wildly as he rams himself into me, the head of his cock practically hitting my cervix with each thrust. Samson wraps my long hair around his fist, holding it like a leash as he jerks me back onto his cock.

I pant with anticipation as I feel him swell within me. He tips over the edge like a storm, slamming his hips against my ass like cracks of thunder, his cum like spurts of hot lighting against the deepest parts of me. My muscles fail me as my arms fall forward, my body sinking into the cold ground. Samson follows me down, pumping the last of his release into me with a sated sigh.

I lay on the cold ground in the forest's quiet stillness, Samson's body resting over me like a victorious conqueror. I've been running for so long, chased by nothing but the ghosts of the past, but now, caught under Samson's weight, pinned against the damp Earth, I feel alive again. My body is exhausted, but something wild within me wants to get up and keep running. I want to run through the woods, take it all in, feel everything instead of running away from it.

Instead, I let Samson's calming, heavy weight anchor me in the present, giving me the freedom to let myself stop fleeing the past.

As soon as he's caught his breath Samson sweeps me into his arms, folding my torn shirt over my chilled skin and carrying me swiftly back to the cabin.

The whole walk back he whispers praise into my ear, telling me how good I was, how he loved my fight, how hot my pussy felt as he slammed into me. He goes straight to the bathroom and stands me up, gently removing all my clothes. Then he examines my scrapes, rinsing them with water to make sure they're only superficial. They are.

Despite my best effort, I think he knows that the true hurt lies much deeper within me.

After the shower Samson directs me to the couch, then adds some of the new wood he chopped this morning into the fire. Staring into it, I feel a flame ignite within me, one that went out so long ago. A new spark of desire settles in my chest, a desire to live, a desire to stop running and let pleasure catch up with me. The heat of the fire comforts me as I watch the flames flicker in the early evening light.

CHAPTER 12

Samson and I sit on the rug in front of the fire with a makeshift charcuterie board and two glasses of wine set between us. We nibble on crackers, cheese, grapes, and nuts in companionable silence. He's dressed in the clothes he arrived in, but I'm wearing an oversized sweatshirt with nothing underneath. I'm so comfortable in his presence that I start getting nervous again, wondering why I didn't feel the need to get dressed. It feels like more of me is bared to him than just my body.

Leave it to me to corrupt this temporary happiness while I'm still in the freaking middle of it.

My nebulous feelings about Samson enshroud the weekend in a growing cloud of anxiety. I feel myself growing attached as each orgasm, each kind moment, weaves new threads into this tether between us. I take a deep breath, attempting to get myself back to the relaxation I felt a minute ago.

"I can hear you thinking over there," Samson ribs, knocking my arm with his elbow.

"I'll think as loudly as I like in my own cabin, thank you very much."

"Is it… just yours?"

I can tell he's trying not to upset me, but we're veering into upsetting territory.

"Yup, it's mine," I answer. His brow furrows further, but I don't explain.

"Okay, okay, you don't want to elaborate, I get it." Samson smiles as he reaches out and pinches my rib. My stomach caves in protectively as I recoil with a laugh.

"So, tell me, how's your whole 'being alone for the holidays' thing working out?"

I give him a playful glare. "Well, I got here Friday afternoon, and you showed up Friday night, so, overall, not as planned."

"You don't think this is better?" Samson responds impishly. "Wouldn't you have gotten a little scared, being this isolated and alone?"

I huff. "Being alone isn't scary. People are. Take right now for example. I'm stuck in a remote cabin, defenseless, with no cell reception and a mysterious, possibly dangerous stranger. This could have been a horror movie."

"If you really thought I was dangerous, then telling me how defenseless and vulnerable you are isn't your smartest move," he laughs. "But I don't think you're actually worried about that, given that you're eating cheese and wine with me in front of a romantic fire."

"Fine," I relent. "But you're still a stranger."

"What do you want to know, then? Although, if I was a bad guy, I'd just lie," he responds with a wink. I glare, and he gives me another infuriatingly sexy smirk.

"Last name? For safety purposes?"

"Nicholas."

"Shut up. No, it is not."

"What? You think I'm lying about my last name? Although, I did say if I was evil, I'd lie," he winks.

"That's not reassuring, you know. And that's a first name."

"Things can be multiple things."

"How philosophical. But seriously, that's your last name? Samson

Nicholas sounds like the perfect alias for Santa, if he were in witness protection or something."

"Well, then it's a shitty alias, since you figured me out in the first 60 seconds you saw me. *'Did you just say, Santa?'*" he jests playfully, imitating my higher voice.

"Yeah, yeah, yeah, laugh it up."

I shove him playfully and he smiles, lunging toward me as he growls, "You're gonna get it," and he rolls on top of me.

"It's my turn to ask a question," he says, his face serious again. I nod. His hands shift to my ribs. "Are." They glide up. "You." He nips at my ear, his mouth hovering there. "Ticklish?" he whispers, immediately tickling my armpits. I squirm and scream in surprise and he laughs, that deep "huh, huh, huh" that makes me melt.

"Stop!" I yelp. "I'm not done with my questions! Stop!"

"Okay, okay," he responds, rolling back off me with a smile. "I'll answer one last question."

"I've only gotten one answer!" He gives me a stern frown and I back down. "Fine, last one. What do you do for work?"

"That's what you ask the man who's been in your bed all weekend? You don't want to know if I'm married? If I'm a criminal? If I've got a dozen illegitimate children spread across the state?" He tickles my side and I fold in on myself, laughing and yelling.

"I take it back! I take it back! I want a redo!"

"Nope," he replies with a bright smile. "No takebacks. I'll answer your question. I used to deliver packages."

"Is that an actual answer, or a Santa joke?"

"It's a vague, but real answer," he says with a roguish smile.

"Wait. Used to? *Used to?*" My hand reaches out to tickle him back, but he catches it in his fist before I can get to him, gently biting my finger before releasing me. "I didn't ask what you *used* to do. I want your current occupational status, sir." His nostrils flare at the term 'sir'. "Are you unemployed, then? Living in a van down by the creek?"

"Which creek?" he laughs. "No, I'm employed, kind of. Self-employed. I've got a couple of businesses in the area. One sells toys, one sells treats."

"You're definitely fucking with me." Cheeky bastard can't stop making Santa jokes.

"Nope. Vague, but true." He smiles, and I stick my tongue out at him in response. Then a though strikes me.

Treats.

"Wait. The dispensary. I saw you pull into the parking lot. There was another biker dude in there, too. Is that the treat store?"

He smiles, shaking his head.

"You're a better detective than I thought. Yes, detective, I confess. That's the treat store."

"Seriously? Oh. My. God. That means… you named the cookies!" I sit up on my knees with my finger pointed at him like I've cracked a big case, but he wasn't there for that discussion, so he looks at me like I'm a loon.

"You… got me?" he answers, his confirmation laced with confusion.

"So then…" I start, thinking over the events of the weekend.

"I can see those wheels turning, baby girl, whatcha spinnin' up in there?"

"All of this is your fault!" I yell, startling Samson, whose expression is more confused than ever. "I bought YOUR cookies, so YOU got me high, which means you're the reason I flung myself at you like a feral monkey!"

"A sexy feral monkey," he laughs. "But yeah, I guess if I'm gonna go down for a crime, I'll gladly take the blame for getting you high, little toy."

"Did you say something about going down somewhere?" I purr, mimicking his little double eyebrow raise. From the smirk on his face, I probably looked deranged doing it.

"Alright, your question time is over," Samson states, sitting up. "But since you can't seem to stop asking more and more, I get one last one."

"I accept your terms," I grumble. "But go grab that last cookie. Let's split it."

"You're bossy this evening," Samson chides as he gets up to grab the paper bag with the last cookie. He snaps it in half and hands a piece to me. His now empty hand veers toward my armpit to tickle me again and I squeak, backing away.

He takes a bite as he sits back down, looking more serious, a distinct shift away from our playful banter into a more sincere tone. "What were you thinking about when we first started eating?"

Well, that's a wet blanket of a question.

"The past, the present, and the future," I reply, sticking out my tongue before shoving the rest of the cookie in my mouth so my mouth is too full to answer.

"Your Christmas references are getting out of control, my little Ghost of Christmas Pussy. Answer the question."

He leans back as he takes a casual bite of his cookie, projecting a vibe that says, 'we're just two people chatting, no big deal'. I did enjoy learning a bit more about him, but that was all surface level stuff, not big deep reveals like this.

Still, I'm not going to forget that I have a weed hook up now. Well, both weed and a hook up, I giggle to myself, amused by how strange my brain gets when I'm resisting being serious.

"So, you get to be vague, but I don't? That's not fair," I complain, the words muffled by the hunks of cookie I'm trying to swallow down.

"You didn't sign up for fair. We're playing by my rules. Now stop being a little brat and tell me, or I'll make your punishment worse."

I swallow the bite in my mouth with a cartoonish gulp.

"So, I'm getting punished either way?" I pout girlishly. His eyes glint, promising all kinds of sexy trouble. My body responds immediately, tingly goosebumps rising on my skin.

"Yes, but if you're a good girl, I'll make it a punishment you'll like." He wraps his hand gently around my throat with a devilish smirk. If the punishment is some light choking, then he's right about me liking it, since I'm already getting turned on.

"What's the punishment?"

"Answer first."

With so many feelings rushing through me amid our playful teasing, I need this sexual release to block all of that out. I glare at him through squinted eyes but relent, giving him a nod and a cheeky thumbs up.

"When did he leave you?"

My eyes widen as my back goes ramrod straight. How could he know that? I guess I let him assume someone cheated on me, so that's what he must mean. Thinking fast, I answer with the truth I'm willing to give.

"About two years ago."

His brow furrows at that. Two years is a long time to still be this messed up over a simple break up, even one with cheating involved. I watch his expression shift from curious and calculating to angry. He's never actually looked dangerous to me, but his clenched jaw and flinty stare give me a taste of what that might be like.

"Did he hurt you? Do I need to kill him?" he asks, each word cutting like a knife.

I can't help it; I bark out a laugh. That's the opposite of what I need. His brow creases.

"No need," I tell him.

"Mm," he responds, relaxing. "You kill 'em?"

My laugh rings out again. "Sure. He's buried in the woods at the back of the property."

"We fucked on your dead ex's grave? That's hardcore, even for me."

"I'm messing with you," I laugh. "I didn't kill him."

A tumor did that. Lots of 'em.

He takes a sip of his wine, staring at me like a puzzle with missing pieces. "Why are you still punishing yourself, then?"

"A cabin full of sex toys, smutty books, and alcohol looks like a punishment to you?"

"Depends."

"Depends on what?"

"On why you're here. On why you're alone in this cabin at Christmastime."

"I'm not, Samson. You're here," I answer, twisting the conversation in my favor, although I think him being here might mean more to me than I want it to. "Can we just enjoy that, for now?"

Samson's jaw twitches at my response, but when he looks deep into my eyes, his steely expression softens. He leans over me, pressing his lips against mine in a passionate, sensual kiss. As much as I wanted a punishment, the soft way Samson gives me this easy affection feels even better.

After several minutes of kissing like hormonal teenagers, he turns to lie on his side next to me with a sated smile. "Okay, little toy. Let's enjoy tonight."

My heartbeat stumbles as he says *tonight*. This our last night. I'm gripped with the sudden urge to know something more about him, something that anchors him in reality so he can't drift away like a figment of my imagination after he leaves.

"One last question, please," I ask sincerely.

"Okay, Mary. I'll give you this one."

"Yesterday you said you had a lot of experience dealing with tough shit. What did you mean by that?"

His face falls so quickly it's like a jolt to my heart. I've been so obstinate about not giving him any of my emotions that I never considered he's got plenty of them swirling around too, past hurts of his own to hide. It hits me that I might not be a car wreck he's slowing down to watch, like the rest of my friends and family, but someone with a similar pain.

"Since you didn't answer my question directly, I'm not going to tell you exactly what happened, but I'll tell you about the circumstances around it."

I nod, desperate now to know if this intense attraction to him is rooted in something else. If it's more like two hurt people finding each other, although I'm not sure what would change if that were true.

"I said I delivered packages, but I, ah, actually led the organization that did that."

Samson uses his arm to push himself up off the floor. With a shake of his head, like he isn't happy he's doing this, he pulls off his t-shirt and turns around, showing me the large tattoo on his back. I'd seen it a couple times, but hadn't had the chance to really study it. Tattoos cover most of his back from his upper shoulders to the waistband of his jeans, and he clearly planned the design.

It looks like the old school tattoos I've seen on bikers in movies and TV shows, but with more Japanese elements. An eagle with spread wings drapes across the top of his shoulders, the top of its head at the base of his neck. Below it, the largest piece by far is a skeleton in a leather jacket riding a motorcycle through Japanese style waves. The motorcycle has licks of flames flaring back from its wheels, and the wave seems to part around the skeleton and bike like Moses.

Other, smaller elements look filled in over time: skulls, a snake, a devil with his tongue out, angel wings, and an eye with a sword through it. The letters "MMC" arc along his lower back to complete the piece. All the imagery is vaguely menacing, but the design comes together in a way that I can only describe as beautiful. Samson turns around, his face heavy with the weight of the answer he's about to give.

"So, you didn't work for UPS," I joke, attempting to break the tension. He lets out one little 'huh' of a laugh. I wish I knew how to cheer him up enough to get his usual three.

"It's an MC, Michigan Motorcycle Club, and for quite a few years, I ran it. My father ran it before me, and I was always going to take it over when he was ready to pass it on. I didn't want it, but nobody asked me if I did or didn't, since it wasn't a choice."

"Probably obvious, but the packages we dealt with weren't legal. Drugs, weapons. We had some good guys in the club, but we worked with a lot of bad people. I always told myself I wasn't as bad as those guys since we just delivered the stuff from point A to point B, but people got hurt. In a few extreme cases, I ordered them to get hurt, but most of the time they got hurt like most people do, accidentally. What messed me up the most, though, was when *my* men got hurt because of *me*, because they followed directions and did what I told them to do. The people I've had to take care of, the hurt that will follow me until the day I die, revolved around that. The worst pain of my life was one of those situations."

I desperately want to say something, anything, to make him feel better. Samson confirmed my inkling that something haunts him, but I don't have the right words to respond. I think through all the trite, unoriginal things people said to me, but none of them fit.

The last thing I want to do is insult his honesty with greeting card bullshit. Instead, I raise my hand, cupping his cheek in my palm. When I feel him melt slightly into my touch, I immediately sink into him, lifting his arms and settling against his chest, his white beard tickling my cheek and his body warm against my skin.

"Is that why you 'used to' do that? Why you run your Santa Claus stores now?"

He releases another 'huh' of a laugh before his expression sobers again.

"Yeah, pretty much, although not that easily. I was tired of being in the business of pain. What I do now, peddling pleasure, is much more enjoyable. But membership is for life, sworn in blood, and being the boss isn't something you just submit a letter of resignation for. We all worked together and shared the profits. If I wanted to get away from the day to day, I needed to contribute a different way. I'd never spent much money other than supporting my kids and funding my ex's shopping habits, so I used my savings to open a couple stores. I tithe a percentage of the profits to the club, and I get to step away without any trouble."

There's a lot packed in there. His ex, his kids, his past, all of it sparking a dozen unanswered questions in my head. I asked him for something real, and he placed his hurt in the palm of my hand, trusting me to help him hold it. Instead of my other, more prying questions, I ask, "How's that been working out?"

"Better," Samson answers, kissing me on the head. I can't decipher why the most unrelatable story anyone has ever told me makes me feel so close to him, so I sit with it, giving myself time to figure out how I feel about that. What I do know is that I respect the hell out of the way he took a crappy situation he didn't ask for and came up with a plan to get where he'd rather be instead. And then he did it. It gives me a twinkle of hope that it's not too late to do my version of that.

We only have a short time left, maybe even just tonight, so I promise myself to just enjoy it. I've been so dead set on using Samson as a fantasy that I didn't see there might be a fantasy in here that he needs to play out too. I take his hand, twining his fingers with mine, and commit, for this one last night, to making this cabin a soft place to land for two people who know what it's like to have landed in a hard one.

"There's a hot tub out back," I offer. "Want to go watch the stars?"

Samson looks in my eyes, a thousand potential things to say twinkling within them, but he only nods, squeezing my hand and helping me up.

CHAPTER 13

Samson lifts me in his arms and carries me behind the house. He sets me on the small wooden deck that surrounds the hot tub and strips my clothes from my body slowly and reverently. His eyes track his movements as he unwraps my body, but mine are on the sky. It shines brightly with constellations, the view so clear compared to my city one. Does the sky always have this many stars? I look toward the dark woods, remembering my decision to change the reason I'm running, to find something to run *to* instead of letting the past chase me away from anything new.

My naked body shivers in the cold air, and then I shiver again as Samson's strong, warm arms lift me into the hot tub. My eyes, ever pining, watch each movement of his strong, nimble hands as he undresses himself next, baring his naked body to me in the moonlight.

Samson steps up into the hot tub, his thighs spreading himself open to me as he sinks into the steaming water. I swim into his lap, my thighs spread open on top of his. One of my hands reaches to his cock and the other to his face. I hold him, stroke him, let us soak in whatever alchemy of fate brought us together for this short time. When Samson lets his head fall back in a deep moan, I release a grateful sigh of my own, moving my hand to grip his hair as our chorus of pleasure disperses into the night.

His breath hitches and he lifts his hips, shifting us to fit together more comfortably. I rub my core against his shaft, our wet bodies gliding over each other like they did this morning in the shower. It's his turn to grip my hair, and he does, gathering the wet strands plastered to my shoulders and wrapping the length around his fist. I let myself submit to Samson, my body pliant as he uses his hips and hands to grind our bodies against each other. He rubs my pussy against his cock at his own pace and his eyes shine as bright as stars as he watches where we meet. I roll my hips into him, arching my chest toward his mouth. He teases my nipple with his tongue, then pulls it into his mouth, sucking and swirling. His hands settle on my ribs and his face settles into my neck to kiss me.

"I've spent enough time lying in sin, Mary, to know when I have something holy in my hands. Maybe there's some absolution for me, if I could leave someone better than I found them instead of worse. I might be going to hell, but tonight your thighs spread open on me feel like heaven."

My body sinks down against him, soft where he is hard, two broken halves coming together into something whole, something holy. He presses into me until his hips meet my thighs and my pussy opens to him as he fills me. Our bodies rise and fall together, our hands and mouths worshipping each other's as water laps against us from the waves rippling to the rhythm of our bodies.

I lift my head up, offering my pleasure to the stars as a question. Asking the universe if this offering she's given me, this man in my cabin and in my body, is a guiding star to a new journey. Draping my hands around his neck, my mouth meets his in a deep, slow kiss as I let myself revel in everything happening between us. Samson shifts his body, thrusting at an angle that has me calling out, begging and praising in equal measure.

"Yes, angel. Sing for me. Sing so loud the stars hear what it sounds like when you come."

"Harder, then," I whisper. "Fuck the song out of me."

The only sounds after that are splashing water and my hymns of delicious pleasure as Samson grips my hips and pounds into me. I quiet as the wave of my orgasm crashes over me, my mouth open in a wide O, a silent crescendo as I unravel against him. His roar replaces my song as he follows me, slamming our bodies together with the bruising grip of his fingers holding my ass as the wave of his climax falls over him.

We don't move afterward, our bodies cocooned together, both staring at the stars for answers to questions our bodies already understand, maybe ones that our hearts are starting to comprehend, too.

When our skin gets too wrinkly, we head inside. Samson dresses me in pajamas and I let him, accepting his need to take care of me. Holding my hand, he leads me to the couch and I spread out, draping my feet over his legs after he sits down next to me. The fire warms me as he pulls my fairy tale book from the table beside the couch and reads. His deep voice blends with the crackling of the fire and I feel my eyes close. His voice fades away into the quiet of sleep. All I feel is the warmth of the fire blanketing both of us, blazing through the darkness of the losses that we share, the broken parts that call to each other in the night.

———

Samson's tongue between my thighs wakes me up in the morning. I reach down, running my fingers through his hair, stroking the white and grey strands as his tongue swirls and glides along my pussy. Then I'm gripping his hair, pressing him into me while he swirls his tongue over my clit. Finally, he sends me crashing into a shattering orgasm that breathes life into my sleepy body.

I rub the sleep out of my eyes, unsure what today will look like. Samson has made no references to the future, no promises or assurances. As I raise my arm in a stretch, I reaffirm my decision to savor this gift until it's gone and not be greedy for more.

Too much of a good thing is a real concept, right? Too many cookies make you sick. Too many toys make a child less likely to appreciate any of them. Too much of Samson… the concept feels like a lie in my mouth, but I swallow it anyway, unwilling to admit how bitter it tastes.

I attempt to pull his heavy body up to me, my fingernails digging into his shoulders as I tug, a small whine filtering out of my sleepy mouth.

"Tell me, Mary. Tell me what you need."

"I need you inside of me. Please."

He moves up my body until we're aligned. He grinds his pelvis against me, moving down along my slit, then parting me as he grinds back upwards. He notches himself at my entrance and I gasp.

"This is what you want?"

I nod my head over and over desperately.

"It's what I want, too," he growls as he buries himself all the way inside me in one deep, powerful push. I close my eyes, focusing on the way our bodies come together as Samson continues his slow, shallow thrusts.

On Friday and Saturday, his words and actions shocked me with their dominance, the way they made me want every dirty thing he did to me. Something shifted last night. As he rocks into me now, I'm taken by the sweetness, the gentleness with which he worships my body. He strokes my hair as he kisses me with languid, passionate strokes of his tongue. My body melts into the bed, relaxing as his gliding strokes into my pussy come easier and easier, my body settling into the pleasure.

I wrap my legs around him, pulling him as close to me as possible until Samson's hips meet my inner thighs, and he pauses as he seats himself fully inside of me.

"Open your eyes," he whispers, his thumb stroking against my cheek.

I open them, sighing contentedly as I look at his face, somehow so familiar to me in such a short time. He told me about Boss Samson last night, the man who commanded an entire motorcycle club. The person staring down at me now is the man who lives underneath all that, who wants to give pleasure more than pain.

"You're perfect, Mary. You fit me perfectly."

Samson shifts his position, entering me from a higher angle. I let out a low, groaning moan as his shaft stimulates my clit in a way I've never felt from penetration before. He rocks into me and my body follows his involuntarily, rocking back against him, increasing the friction against my swollen clit. My eyes grow wide as I feel the deep, intense pressure.

"You deserve this, Mary. You deserve all the pleasure this world has to offer. I hope you know that. I hope you believe that."

He said something similar last night, but it sinks in deeper today. Unshed tears glisten as the sensations and emotions overwhelm me. We let our bodies speak, my breasts arching upwards as Samson keeps himself deep inside of me, grinding his pubic bone into my vulva, stimulating my inner walls and my clit simultaneously. He directs the force of his body into my pelvis, his weight pressing against my clit as he rocks into me. My pleasure builds, a pressure in my clit that has me arching further, rubbing myself against him harder. I scratch at his back for purchase, holding him to me as much as he holds me to him. When I meet his gaze, I see the affection written on his face.

"You're taking me so well, Mary. Rub that little clit against me. I need to feel you coming around my cock. Fuck. I need it."

He wraps his arms around me, holding me as my moans get louder and more insistent. All his body weight sinks into me, the pressure on my clit becoming so intense I don't know how much more I can take. My moans deepen, guttural grunts escaping my body as he presses harder, little grinding pulses moving deep within me and against my clit.

"Just like that, Mary. You're doing so good. Your pussy is so good. Let go now, baby. Let it all go."

Samson continues praising me as my grunts echo through the room until I'm crying out, squeezing rhythmically around his cock and pulling him as deep as he can fit while my clit pulses against his base. I feel him swell within me as I clench around his cock in waves until he's grunting too. His hot cum coating deep within me sets off a second wave of my orgasm. He grips me, holding my body against him as we continue to grind our orgasms into each other.

He keeps holding me, kissing the top of my head, my cheeks, my throat. My thoughts threaten to wander back into doubts and anxieties, but the weight of him anchors me in the present. We stay that way, wrapped up in each other, until his weight on me becomes too much.

"Can't breathe, need to tap out," I wheeze with a smile, playfully slapping his back twice to signal him to lift.

"Fuck, sorry," he responds immediately, slinking down my body. As his cock slides out of me, I feel emptiness, but he doesn't leave. His head sinks between my thighs, caressing me with the flat of his tongue. "You have no idea how good your pussy looks like this, freshly fucked and open. Your pussy is magic."

He licks my folds, cleaning away my arousal, keeping the pressure light enough that it's not too much for my sore clit. "God," he grumbles, "You taste even better." His rich, low voice is so soothing that my head falls back on the bed, letting the deep rumble wash over me. I revel peacefully in his attention until I feel his grip tighten on my thighs, his fingers pressing in enough to bruise.

"What's your favorite Christmas dessert, little toy?"

"Cookies," I answer. I feel his come drip out of me.

Oh, fuck.

"Pie," he growls. "Mine is pie."

"So fucking delicious. Here, I'll show you." He reaches two fingers inside of me, thrusting his fingers through our releases, then curls them, dragging his cum out. His fingers move to my mouth, and I open, sucking his fingers and our joined release.

"Swallow, little toy."

Fuck me, but I do. I swallow, then open my mouth, sticking my tongue out so he can see that I did. He presses his fingers back into my mouth, against my tongue, and I close my mouth around them, swirling my tongue and sucking again.

"Mm. My little Christmas angel has a dirty fucking mouth, doesn't she?"

He sinks his finger further into my mouth and I gag as he presses down, but I don't dare jerk away. My breath hitches as he pulls his finger back, hooking it against the side of my lips to pull my mouth open.

"Such a good girl, swallowing everything I gave you. I bet you want more, don't you? You want whatever I give you."

With his finger hooked in my mouth, I can't speak, so I nod enthusiastically

I try to imagine what happens when I get back to Chicago. Is sex after forty going to be like this? This weekend has been so intense that I've only read about things like this in my filthiest, smuttiest books. If I'm being honest, if Will had tried this shit, I probably would have either slapped him or laughed him out of the bed. I would have thought I was too old for this. Too… I don't know, normal for this. This kind of filth was for lithe twenty something's in sex clubs, not widowed ex-HR managers in their forties. I didn't have the body or the intense sexuality that inspired this kind of behavior.

But as Samson spits into my hooked open mouth and then nudges my jaw closed with his knuckle, I feel that power radiating through me again. Maintaining eye contact as I swallow, a carefree laugh escapes my lips, and I feel more powerful, more sexual, than ever. I feel fucking invincible, I realize. I've been underestimating myself.

"I'm going to keep feeding you and filling you all day, little toy. This day is mine. You are mine."

Warmth radiates inside of me as he tells me he's planning to stay today. It's just for the weekend, I remind myself, but fuck if I won't enjoy the hell out of it.

I nod. "Yes, Santa."

"Take your time getting up, I'm going to make breakfast."

CHAPTER 14

smile as I step into the kitchen to see a mug of coffee and plate of scrambled eggs on toast. Between this and the charcuterie last night, it's clear that Samson isn't a big chef. Still, the simple, hearty breakfast sets off a brief pang in my chest. I miss having someone else to do simple things like make breakfast with me. We chat as we eat, but both of our eyes are brimming with wanton intent as we stare at each other across the table. As soon as the food is gone, we're immediately back in the bedroom and wrapped up in each other.

If my pussy doesn't survive all of this action, I'll be eternally grateful that she took one for the team. Took a *lot* for the team.

Samson's dominance hasn't faded, but the way we explore each other's bodies has turned languid and equal. Today everything is on the table, and we feast on each other's pleasure like gluttons let loose on each other, uncaring of the ache coming when the buffet ends. I want to feel Samson's presence everywhere and I tell him so, which is how I end up on my hands and knees, gasping as his fingers pull out of my tight ring of muscles, a cold stream of lube dripping onto my ass. He places his cock right where his fingers just exited.

"Breathe, little toy. Press back into me. Let me in."

"Tuok," I whine. "I don't think I can take it."

"Haven't you realized how much you can take? How much you can handle? Push through this. I'll make it feel so good."

Samson reaches around me, his fingers circling my clit. He guides me through each breath, coaching me until the head of his cock sinks in past the tight rim of my ass. It's been years since I last did this, but this morning I want Samson in every inch of me before he leaves.

He rewards my trust, giving my body time to accommodate him, entering me inch by burning inch so that by the time he sinks fully into me, the intense pressure has already started morphing into the unique pleasure of taking him where my body tells me he shouldn't go.

My body is a fool, and I'm worried my heart is too as he sinks dangerously deep. He spreads across my skin and my soul like glitter, never fully disappearing. I imagine I'll be finding memories of him for years to come.

Samson winds me up like a toy as I press back into his hips feverishly until I'm wound so tight there's nowhere to go but to come completely undone.

"Fuck, fuck. You take me so well," Samson growls as I feel thick ropes of heat deep within me as he comes.

The filthy, foreign sensation sets me off in a chain reaction. I shove Samson's hand out of the way as I explode next, circling my clit feverishly as my tight channel milks out the last of his release. When we're done, Samson brings us both to the shower where he cleans my body reverently. Our lips tangle together under the warm water, pressing confessions into each other's mouths with our tongues, silent secrets we can only reveal like this.

After we dry off, we settle back into bed. My body is clean of his touch, and I need it back on me, need him to cover me with his hands and his tongue. Morning drifts into the early afternoon as neither of us speak about what is coming, focusing only on the way our bodies come together. I memorize his expressions and sounds as we pleasure each other, broaching each other's bodies, but not the future.

The pleasure shifts to pain as we glide into the afternoon, our bodies sore, dehydrated, and raw. Holding back the dam of my emotions becomes too much to bear, and I can feel it boiling under the surface. The shift last night, the decision to let myself be free with him for as long as this lasts, has morphed to an intimacy I'm not prepared to address.

All at once I feel the panic rising again. My heart pumps and my skin flushes as I realize how this fantasy has shifted into something real. He didn't barrel into me all at once, he just kept making small advances, tiny cracks that deepened and deepened until I ended up here, wanting to see him again after today. My cheeks flush as I think about what I want in this moment. I want his phone number. I want to know about the kids he mentioned in passing last night. I want to see if he has plans for New Year's.

My fists clutch onto the bed, all my muscles going tense as my panic rises further. Samson lifts onto his elbows as he notices my clenched expression.

"What's wrong?" he asks, his voice full of genuine concern. It was comforting before, but today it upsets me how well he can read me, how he seems to know what's happening inside me when he was never supposed to get that far. "Mary, are you okay?"

"No, I'm not, Samson. Your x-ray vision can't see that already?" I bark. My reaction feels extreme, but I can't rein in the panic breaking out within me as my palms sweat and my chest starts to hurt.

"I see it, Mary. That's why I stopped," Samson answers, his voice calm but his face tense. "I'm asking you *what* is wrong. I just want to help."

"And over and over I've made it clear I don't want to talk about it, Samson. From the first moment I jumped on your dick, I've made it clear that I *do* want to fuck you, and I *don't* want to talk about the past, or my ex, or any of my shit. Why do you keep pushing me?"

"Mary," he growls.

"I mean it! What is it? Pity? An easy opportunity to get laid? Why did you stay?" I back away, unable to handle how close I feel to him.

"What's your game, Samson? Does it get you off to fuck the sad, lonely woman? You want me to share my shitty, traumatic past so you can feel like a good guy?"

None of my words are fair, but life isn't fair, either. It hasn't been fair for me. I played the game by the rules, and I still lost. Grasping on to the panic, I unleash my anger because letting that spill out of me keeps me from spilling the truth.

"Mary," Samson repeats sternly, frustration simmering under the surface of his controlled words. "I didn't stay this weekend so I could fuck some sad woman, or whatever the fuck." His hand waves in the air, swatting my angry words away like flies.

"I stayed because I wanted to fuck *you*. There's something here, Mary, something about you that drew me in. Why would I stay this long if I just wanted some easy fuck? You're not some chick to pity, or some sad woman to exploit. Maybe that's how you see yourself when you look in the mirror, or when you talk to your friends, but that's not what everyone else sees. That's not what I see."

I storm around the room, pulling clothes on despite the anger vibrating through me. Samson watches me like I'm a wounded animal lashing out, which is the truth, but I never let myself do this before. I stayed sad about what happened to me. I never let myself get angry about it.

Samson gets dressed too, keeping his distance.

"What do you see, then, Samson? A little toy, a little broken piece of plastic you think you can fix? I didn't ask you for that."

"I don't know what I'm fucking looking at, Mary. I see the hurt, though, and believe me, I know that feeling. Tell me. Please, tell me. Tell me what I'm looking at."

I've spent the entire weekend holding back this last piece of me, this place where my soul tore the worst, and I don't want to let him have it right before he walks out the door. Which he's going to, because I'm acting completely insane. More than that, I know something happened to him, too, and that scares me worse. It terrifies me, the idea of what might happen if we hold our broken pieces up to each other's, that they might match and form something new, something hopeful. What happens to that piece of me when he drives away?

Is this my destiny, to collect the memories of these perfect men and carry their ghosts with me? How do you escape the ghosts when the place that's haunted is your body? Your heart?

"Mary," he says again, his pleading voice so soft and comforting that my anger sparks along my skin, his words scraping me like a match.

Already he's treating me differently, like something breakable, like one false step and I'll shatter. I don't want that from him. It doesn't fit the fantasy I had for us this weekend. You don't take a piece of porcelain out in the woods and fuck her into the dirt. You don't slam glass up against the front door and hold it there by the throat.

Fine.

If he wants to know so badly, I'll shatter myself. I'll shatter whatever is between us, because this is the end, right? Everyone sees me as broken anyway, so why not Samson too?

"You really want to know what's wrong? My husband is DEAD. What you're looking at is a widow. A woman who, at age thirty-eight, watched her husband deteriorate so quickly that I was making fun of his costume on Halloween and staring at a flat line before we even hit Thanksgiving because his heart was too full of tumors to keep beating."

"Mary, I..."

"Stop, Samson. You wanted to know and now you do, even though I didn't want this. Didn't want to see the fucking pity on your face like everyone else's. I wanted one weekend where I wasn't a widow, where someone would look at me and just see Mary. You did that, and *fuck,* I really liked it. I like the way you look at me, Samson. I didn't want you to see the truth that everyone else sees. That I see. The tragic woman whose husband died. But, fine." It's my turn to swat at the air. I wave his words away, wave this weekend away, wave him away.

"Now you see it too, and there's no going back. The fantasy had to end sometime, right?" I choke out a painful laugh.

Samson rushes up to me, his breath heavy. He tries to place his hands on my shoulders, but I brush them off, crossing my arms. He turns away, raking his fingers through his hair, before circling back to me.

"I get it, Mary. That's what I've been trying to show you this whole time. I understand. Do you know what people see when they look at me? What everyone I know sees? They see the man who killed his brother. The leader who sent his little brother off to a sketchy fucking deal that ended with his stiff body lying dead in a parking lot. That's what I see. That's what my MC sees. I have to stare at that man in the mirror every fucking day, and then I have to live anyway."

My breath escapes me in a sob. The tears pour out of me as the anger slips into the ocean of hurt below it. Samson pulls me into his arms and I'm helpless to fight it, my tears and pain puddling on his red shirt as I stand there.

"My brother, Cole, he didn't die for no reason. I can't believe that. It happened, no matter what, whether I tell everyone or no one. But I still have to live after that. I have to make new decisions. I still see the man who gave those orders and then got that goddamn nightmare of a call hours later, but I see new versions of myself too. Ones that might not have happened if I didn't turn the pain into something good."

"I don't know how to do that," I stammer.

"It doesn't happen overnight. The past still happened. You pay your respects to it, but you do your best to imagine a better future than the present you're living in, and then you do the hard fucking work until it's real, until it's right in front of your eyes."

"Did it work?" I ask, and he nods. "What do you see now?"

"I see a man who makes legal money instead of dirty money, who sells shit that makes people happy. I see a man who lost his wife and kids because he was too married to his club to make them a priority. But I also see myself bringing takeout to my daughter every Tuesday night. I see myself at the bar on the weekend, eating wings with my son and watching the game. I didn't turn into a saint, but I can fall asleep at night."

"That sounds nice," I croak, my voice hoarse from crying. Samson squeezes me in his thick arms, planting a kiss on the top of my head.

"I'm sorry he died, Mary. Your husband. What was his name?"

"Will," I answer in a wobbly whisper.

"I'm so fucking sorry Will died, Mary. You didn't want to tell me, but I knew. I didn't have a name or explanation for it, but I saw your pain." He takes my face between his large, calloused hands. "I saw the rest too, the other parts of you. They're still there. There's more to come for you, okay?"

My breath catches on another sob. Pounding my fist hard against Samson's chest, I tell him the truth of it.

"It hurts, Samson. It hurts so fucking bad. But most of the time, I'm more scared of feeling good again, of what that means. What does that make me, if his death doesn't hurt anymore? I'm already getting used to it. I don't think I can let it slip away."

"It's been almost 15 years since Cole died, and I can say with absolute confidence that you don't need to worry about that. It doesn't go away, but it changes."

"Well, you're the elder grieving person, I guess," I respond with a joyless laugh. "When does it get better? Easier?"

"I'm the elder everything to you," he jokes solemnly. "But easier? Never. And also, really fucking slowly. The thing is, and I'm sure you know this, but each time you feel a little better, that fucks you up a bit, too. It feels like a betrayal for it to get easier to handle. Over time, that guilt has become less and less brutal. It still hurts that Cole's gone, but it's made me stop to think, to feel things I never bothered to when I thought I was invincible. Now, when there's a sunny day to ride my bike, or I watch a team win with my kid, I let myself sink into it. I'm not gonna let myself miss out on the good things happening now because of the things I lost before."

Leaning into Samson's broad, powerful chest, I try to absorb his words. I'd been feeling down, knowing he was leaving, but I should know better. Everything ends. The only thing I can do is enjoy it now.

"You want to tell me about Will?"

I wipe the tears away, a little smile forming on my lips as I think about Will the person instead of Will the tragedy.

"He was a runner. The kind of guy who did a Turkey Trot at 6 am on Thanksgiving, whereas my version of a Thanksgiving morning is getting the turkey in the oven and watching the parade with some coffee. My point is, he was healthy. Or he looked like it. So, when he started having symptoms of something being wrong in September, the doctors didn't take it seriously.

"He was doing his normal morning runs, but he was getting tired more quickly than usual. We joked about it- how he was getting old, how age was affecting both of us. Then he started losing some weight, his heart rhythm was off on his smart watch, and he was having chest pain on and off. The doctor said it was probably stress, but they set us up for testing at the end of October. By the time he went in for testing, we knew it couldn't be stress. He was waking up soaked in sweat, getting random fevers, even fainted. That scan led to more, and by the time we got the diagnosis he was already in the hospital. His heart, especially the right atrium, was full of tumors. Cardiac Sarcoma. It's rare, and it's aggressive. Surgery wasn't an option, and when we found out it had spread to other organs, a transplant wasn't either. Most people get months, but his heart failed the week of Thanksgiving."

"Is Thanksgiving a bad holiday too, or just Christmas?"

"I didn't even really register Thanksgiving that year, to be honest, so it didn't hurt as bad. By Christmas we'd had the funeral, and I was still in shock, but not the same way I was those first weeks. It was the first holiday around other people, the first real holiday without Will. It was my introduction to what it would be like for me out in the world without him."

Samson wraps his arms around me more tightly. "I remember how that feels, to go back out in the world as this completely different person, with all this random new shit that bothers you. It feels like there's a permanent part of me that associates things with death that normal people wouldn't."

"Yeah. It's hard to explain if you haven't been through it. So, thank you. You didn't have to listen to all this. But I'm glad you did."

As I say it, I realize I mean it. I am glad he knows. I've been in denial, dead set on denying any feelings towards Samson. Even though I was instantly drawn to him, I tried to keep him out. Thought it would be easier. But it's actually easier to know there's other people out there dealing with the same thing I am. I feel more connected, less alone.

"Sometimes you don't need someone to fix things, you just need them to listen. My daughter taught me that," he smiles. "I keep trying to make up for lost time, make everything better for her, but she just wants to talk to her dad."

"I know, but sometimes I wish someone *could* fix this. I've talked to a therapist about it ever since it happened. Now, like you said, I want to feel something else. Let the bad somehow help me appreciate the good."

"I can't fix it, but I can try to show you. Help you figure out how to use the pain."

"I want that. I want to try."

CHAPTER 15

Samson gently helps me out of my clothes, directing me to my hands and knees on the bed. I feel so raw, so exposed with my body and my pain on display. But I need to try, to allow someone to see my pain and help me figure out how to mold it into something new.

"Are you ready, Mary?"

I take a deep breath. "Yeah, I am."

"You trust me?"

I do. More than you know. More than I should.

"Yes."

"We're going to use colors instead of a safe word, okay? Red for stop completely, yellow for slow down or take a break. Green for yes, keep going."

"Okay," I answer, liking the simplicity of that.

"What color are you right now, Mary?"

"Green."

"Good," he answers, rubbing my back. "Whatever happens is fine, alright? I've got you. Focus on your body, what you feel. Sink into it."

As if I wasn't already hyperaware of every sensation right now.

"I hear you. Less talkie, more fixie," I joke, trying to get this started so I can release the shaken pop bottle feeling in my chest. Samson lets out a small huff, a wicked little laugh full of promise. He leans over, placing a gentle kiss on my forehead, then walks behind me.

A heavy slap lands on my ass cheek, erasing the smile from my face as all my thoughts focus in on the sensation. Another palm follows right on top of it, changing the tingling sensation from the first slap into a burning sting. My thoughts focus in on his hands, and the only question in my mind becomes where the next slap will land. His palm cracks against the back of my thigh and I fall forward with a grunt, my cheek pressing into the bed as I try to recover my breathing.

"My little toy," Samson whispers from behind me. "It's okay. Sometimes it takes a few whacks to get a broken toy working again. Let's see if that works. I'm gonna try six. Count them for me."

A stinging slap hits my left ass cheek. I release a whine as it vibrates through me.

"Color?"

"Green," I exhale.

"Good, because I told you to count," Samson growls. "It only counts if I hear you say it."

He hits the same spot again, and I yelp. "Two!"

"One, naughty girl," he responds. "First one didn't count."

He continues spanking me, his slaps landing randomly around my ass and the backs of my thighs. The heat of the sting morphs into a burn of arousal. Samson's hands follow each slap, caressing over each spot. He wipes the pain away, leaving only pleasure in its wake. His slaps move up my inner thighs, and by four and five I'm rocking into them, my yelps turning to moans. His last slap shocks me as it lands directly against my wet pussy, forcing out a scream.

"SIX!"

Instead of caressing me, he sinks two fingers into me once he's done. I release a long, guttural moan as they enter me. My eyes are wide, my body confused by the mixture of pain and pleasure. Is this yellow? I trust Samson, and I want to see where this goes. Can I trust myself? Moaning deeply, I rock into him as his thick fingers pump in and out.

"Color?"

All I can think about is the way he strokes me. I need his thick fingers exactly where they are.

"Green!"

"Mm," he responds, pleased. "Only a naughty girl would be this wet from being spanked. You liked that."

I moan in response, but it isn't what he wants. Another spank lands on my outer thigh.

"Yes, Santa. I liked it. I love it."

Samson growls when I call him Santa, his fingers moving harder within me. He curls his fingers, hitting the exact right spot.

"You like how good it hurts, little toy?"

"Yessssss," I moan, sinking the back of my thighs against his hips.

Samson pulls his fingers out of me, and I whine at how empty I feel. I'm so tired of feeling empty. For the past two years I've been an empty shell. I need to feel something else.

He reaches around me, hovering over me as he moves his fingers to my clit, gliding my wetness around the swollen bud in firm circles.

"You like the pain, Mary?"

"Mm," I respond, too focused on my building climax for words.

"You're used to it, aren't you?" he muses.

My heart rate picks up at his statement, at the truth. I'm too close to my orgasm to respond. His fingers pause their circles to grip me, pinching my clit between his fingertips. I gasp as my back bows from the intensity of his touch. Samson uses the momentum to grab the back of my hair, pulling my body upright against him.

"You're accustomed to pain. It's how you think you're supposed to feel, so you've gotten used to it."

He releases my hair and I exhale a deep breath, relieved, until he moves that hand to my breast and pinches my nipple between his fingers. I keen in his arms, resting my cheek against his shoulder. A part of me wants to resist, to wriggle out of his grip, but I sink into the delicious pain instead. His fingers tighten as I arch my chest.

"You think you deserve this, over something you couldn't control. You sink into the pain because you're scared about what happens when it's over."

Samson grips my hips, pressing me against his, the cold metal of his belt buckle fitting perfectly against my slit. The cool, smooth loop feels so good that I grind myself against it, desperate for release. It sinks inside my lips, rubbing against my clit. His hands move up the center of my body, from my belly to my throat, feeling the way my body tenses from the sensations. Samson pushes my upper body forward, pressing his palm into my cheek to pin me to the mattress.

"Your body knows the truth, Mary. Feels what you don't want to admit to yourself."

He releases my head, moving both of his hands to my core. Two fingers enter me, curling and stroking upward. Two more move to my clit, circling and circling, spiraling me up toward an explosion that only he can detonate.

"There's pleasure waiting for you after the pain. Pleasure made even sweeter because you survived the rest. You didn't ask for this kind of pain, little toy. You didn't deserve it, either, but you got it anyway."

He pinches my clit again and I moan, begging incoherently until he soothes it away with his swirling fingers.

"It's okay to want the pleasure waiting for you afterwards. Even if you don't think you deserve it, it's okay to want that. Release the pain, Mary. Even for just this moment, let yourself experience what comes after it."

At some point, under the pain and pleasure his hands deliver, my moans have turned to sobs.

"Color," Samson immediately demands. I'm grateful that he does, but I want this. Need it so bad.

"Green, green, green," I pant, tears collecting on the quilt below me.

I'm rocking my hips into his fingers, my head pressing into the mattress as my sobs rush out with each thrust and swirl until my body unravels. Clenching and throbbing, screaming and sobbing, my orgasm releases, filling the room. Samson's hands continue moving until my body falls flat onto the bed.

The quilt is damp below me as I lie there, my body shaking and crying. Samson gathers me into his arms like a child, moving us so he's sitting against the headboard and I'm lying on his chest. I rest against him, feeling the gentle movements of his hands on my back as my breathing calms.

"Thank you," I whisper.

He kisses the top of my wild, messy hair.

"I'm not telling you to never be sad, Mary, to never feel the pain. Just don't stay stuck there, baby."

Baby.

Why does that sound so right? I release a deep moan as I sink into his body, a moan direct from my lungs, only one organ away from my heart.

"That," he says, stroking my back. "That's what I want. You implied earlier that I wanted to fuck a sad woman, but that's not it. I want your desire, your pleasure. This goddess of a woman hiding in a shell of pain. I don't want to fuck some sad woman; I want to fuck the sadness *out* of you. Like just now, when you were sobbing under my fingers while you came. I want your tears flowing from my dick thrusting down your throat. I want you wailing from my cock pounding so hard into you. I want you dying a hundred small deaths underneath me, and then I want to keep bringing you back to life after each one. There's a part of you that fell asleep when he died. You've been alive, but not living."

I sit up to face him, buzzing with adrenaline as I recover from the dramatic comedown. I smile as I realize I do want to feel it all, as the endorphins make me feel light and floaty.

"It is aliiiiiive," I say in a mock Dr. Frankenstein voice, pressing my naked body against his clothes.

"She lives!" he responds in the same, silly voice. "I think reanimation is more of a Halloween thing, though." He pinches my side, winking at me.

"No, this is definitely a Christmas story," I assert, looking around the room with a grin. "Snowy cabin, starry nights, Santa coming to visit. Definitely Christmas. And Santa did great with my gifts, even though I didn't make a list."

"I told you, Mary, you deserve it."

As I snuggle against him, I see the sun fading in the sky. I assume he needs to work at his stores tomorrow, that this is it.

"I asked you before, but I'm still curious, what did I kidnap you away from this weekend? What's next for Samson, toy store owner and secret Santa?"

"Mm, that's vaguely accurate," he grins, still needling me. "You know, just going back to being a side character instead of the main one."

"You don't want to be the main character in your own life?"

"I've ended up the main character in a lot of stories I didn't want any part of. Now I'm a supporting character, and I like it."

"But look at you," I answer with a laugh. "You're going to be the star of the show in any room you enter. Why would you fight that?"

"I've had enough of it. A lot of the stories are written on my skin, to remind me why I chose this path."

He shifts me to his side so I can see him. Lifting his left arm, he reveals a circular scar on his triceps. It's my first time seeing one, but it's obviously a bullet wound. "This kind of story." He turns, showing me a long, raised scar on his right side, just under his ribs. "This kind of story." He points at the tattoo just to the right of his heart. Black and white angel wings spread over the name Cole encircled by a halo. "And especially this kind of story."

"I'm sorry. I know. But it's like you told me. It's not over yet. Your story isn't over."

"You really want to hear what my days are like? My boring, average daily routine?" Samson asks me in that deep, penetrating voice. Yes, I want to hear it. I'd listen to that voice read the phone book, but I actually do want to know this.

"I really really do," I respond.

"I get up early. I go to the gym, work out for a couple of hours. Shower. I head to one of my shops to see what they need from me. Usually, it's nothing. I put the right people in charge, and they do a good job. I'll sit in my office, looking over the documents and the spreadsheets, and they'll all look good. The manager, who's half my age, will pitch me an idea and nine times out of ten, it's good. Something I wouldn't have thought of. Maybe after that I'll check on the other store, but it'll be the same."

"Isn't that good? You built something successful."

"Yeah, it is. It is. After all my fuckups, things somehow turned out good. I'm not sure I'm worthy of it, but they did."

"You are. You deserve it, Samson. You deserve all the good things."

He looks at me, hearing his own words thrown back at him. It's difficult to accept the same encouragement we give easily to others. He pulls me under his arm again.

"A couple times a week, I see my kids after work. They're grown now. We're closer than I could have hoped for, even though I missed a lot more than I should have. They didn't know me well enough when they were little, and after their mom left, they hated me because she did. I don't blame them for that, but I'm trying to make up for it. Trying to accept that they turned out good. They're fantastic, actually. Flawed like the rest of us, but great, and I don't deserve credit for it. When I was younger, I thought they belonged to me, my family. Trophies I could bring out when I wanted to and then put back on a shelf while I did whatever else I made my priority over them. But they belong to themselves. I've created all these things, my kids, my businesses, and none of them need me. I'm proud of them, but they're not mine anymore. It's okay, though. It's good. After all the bad, I know it's good."

"I know you said they don't need you, but what do you need?" I ask, staring at his soulful blue eyes. His face softens, and he looks down at his lap. When he looks back up at me, there's something new there.

"That's an interesting question, Mary. But fuck if I have an easy answer for it." His eyes are full of words, but I'm not sure he wants them read just yet. "Enough about me, what about you? What's next for you?"

"Well, I think I'll be here the full two weeks I planned. You know, have the alone time I planned for," I joke, and he reaches under my armpits to tickle me.

"Everything else is up in the air. I haven't made any plans in a long time. It felt like a farce to plan for the future when it could all go to shit in an instant. But there are things I think about. Buying a new condo, maybe, one with fewer ghosts. Moving away from Chicago, even. I don't feel tied there anymore. I spend a lot of time volunteering and I really like it, so maybe I could make a job out of that. Maybe writing. I don't know. Everything's been a blank page since Will died, and that used to make me feel sad, but I'm considering now that it might be exciting. I might be… hopeful."

"I like that answer." Samson's eyes sparkle. "I want that for you."

He stands up, grabbing his clothes and putting them on.

"It's almost dinnertime, Mary. I think it's best I get out of your hair. The road looks clear of ice now, so I can get home safe, even with the angry gear."

My brain floods with questions. Wants to know where 'home' is, wants to ask for a phone number, wants… more. But maybe this is okay; how it's supposed to be. I'm supposed to want more of the future and accept the past.

Everything ends eventually, and today is the day that this ends. Us.

I get dressed as well, trailing behind Samson as he moves to the door to put on his boots.

He stands, his hands in his pockets, and looks at me with a warm smile lighting his face. My body vibrates with energy, totally unsettled. How do I say goodbye? I didn't choose my goodbye last time. I'm not really choosing it now, either, but I'm not stopping it. Without the words to say it, I show him.

I launch myself into his arms. He grabs me as I leap into him with an 'oof' as we collide and a deep growl when I press into his mouth. Our kiss is passionate, wild, alive. Two broken people trying to figure out how to put it all back together.

Samson turns, pressing my body into the door, our entire weekend coming full circle with the same feelings, the same frenzy. My entire being screaming *don't go, I don't know why I feel this way, but I need you. I need you to feel this too.*

The intensity shifts as the passion burns deeper between us. Samson moves us to the rug in front of the fire. His heavy body descends into the cradle of my legs. He kisses my hair, my forehead, my cheeks, and then my mouth again. We kiss each other adoringly, all the fight gone and only the tenderness of our connection left. When we both pull back at the same time, Samson looks down at me with a fond smile.

He nods his head at me one more time, his eyes bright.

"Merry Christmas, Mary. May all your wishes come true."

He stands then, and I focus on the sound of the chains of his boots rattling like sleigh bells as he walks further away, each step jingling until the door shuts and all is quiet and calm in the cabin again, everything except the beating of my heart.

I lie there for a long moment, feeling cold, the fire at my back not strong enough to counter the cracking ice within me. Standing in a rush, I whip the front door open. I step onto the concrete front step to see a single track through the slush on the road disappearing north into the forest, the whisper of his gravelly voice wishing me a Merry Christmas a ghost in my ear.

Shutting the door again, I head back to the fire, tossing a few of the logs Samson cut into the hearth. Curling up on the couch, I listen to the crackle and watch the flame take over the fresh wood. I sit there all night, my arms wrapped around my chest as I watch the fire burn through itself. Lonely tears streak down my face as the fire dims. Even as the flames go out, I remember how they started. The fact they're gone doesn't change how bright they burned, because I was there.

I saw it. I felt it. I burned too. And I will again.

CHAPTER 16

I spend Monday and Tuesday alone in the cabin, reading, listening to music, and lying by the fire. At night I have a few drinks and fantasize about the events of Friday night, hoping to hear a knock at the door. It doesn't come, but my toys get me off as I fall into memories of Samson's body and his words. The reality of him fades into fantasy, this cabin and the weekend we spent in it feeling more and more unreal as the days pass.

Wednesday morning comes with a sprinkle of snow. I planned to head into town at some point. More accurately, back to the intersection south of here that functions as a town, an intersection where a cocky biker winked at me less than a week ago. I think about that motorcycle track headed north and consider trekking there instead, knowing there's another town about fifteen miles that way, but I resist. I don't even know where he was going, exactly, and I refuse to stalk the dispensary to see if he shows up.

He could be at the North Pole for all I know. It's going to be Christmas Eve on Friday.

I need a few more groceries and a lunch I didn't cook, so I head south at noon, parking in front of the diner and following a server with a pencil shoved in her gray bun to a booth with a linoleum table and plastic seats.

"Do you have Wi-Fi by any chance?" I ask her after I order a coffee and a club sandwich.

"Oh lord, I know we do, but I wouldn't know how to get you hooked up with it to save my life. Let me see if one of the boys in the kitchen know, they're better with these things. I need to keep a list on top of the DVD player, so I remember how to use it," she laughs.

She brings me a hot, mediocre cup of coffee and I smile as I hear the men in the kitchen giving her crap and her loudly putting them in their place. I miss having people around me. The city never really feels alone, not the way the cabin does now. The server comes to my table a few minutes later with a sticky note that has a list of numbers and letters on it.

"This is the password, hopefully you'll know what to do with it. I'll have your sandwich up in just a couple more minutes."

"Thanks," I tell her. There're three Wi-Fi networks in the area, one called QuikGas679, one called SNthcCo, and one called 87ui640pl. I assume the 'thc' is a reference to Milk and Cookies and the gas station is obvious, so I type the diner's password under the string of letters and numbers and log on, checking my email and replying to holiday texts.

My phone has a weak signal here, but it's enough that halfway through my sandwich a few voicemails come through. I stare out the window as I listen to the messages. I watch the younger biker park outside of the cute little cottage and unlock the front door.

Realization smacks me upside the head. His hair is buzzed short, but I can see that what little is there is a light, silvery blond, almost white. He flips the hand-painted open/closed sign over with a hard slam and enters. I remember what Samson told me about his regular day. How he checks in on the kids running his businesses, not needing him. How his own kids are grown, but he's gotten another chance with them.

Is that biker his son?

I shake my head as I remember when the idea of a biker in my bed was just a fantasy. It's still a fantasy, I suppose, but that fantasy has teeth now. And a gravelly voice, white beard, and a magic tongue. God, I need to get back home to my battery-powered buddies.

I listen to a voicemail from my mom telling me how everyone will start arriving on Thursday, and the annual cookie contest will be on Christmas Eve as usual. She doesn't ask me to reconsider coming, but there's enough passive guilt implied that I get the message. Maybe I should head back, just for Christmas. I could make everyone happy and still have another week up here to relax and decompress.

It'd make my family happy, but what would make *me* happy? Everything I can think of revolves around a tall biker with a salt and pepper beard telling me to do increasingly lewd things, and me agreeing. *Yes, Santa.*

Fuck.

Straightening my shoulders, I let myself own what I need. I'm a sexual woman, a desirable woman, and a woman who needs companionship. I've found that twice, and I'll find it again. Right here at this linoleum table, I set a New Year's resolution. When I get back to Chicago, I'm going to give online dating a real try. I am manifesting a man.

A knock on the wood panel at the top of the booth surprises me, and I look up into the smiling face of a small, wrinkled man who must be at least in his eighties.

When I manifested a man, I didn't mean this.

While I'm increasingly intrigued by the idea of an older man, I still have limits.

The man tips his Vietnam veteran hat at me and smiles. "Hi, I'm Vern. Would you be Mary?"

"Vern!" I smile. "Thank you for getting the cabin together for me, I really appreciate it. It's been great to get out here, finally."

"Well, that's just lovely, young lady. That's a nice, sturdy cabin there, was a shame to see it sit empty for so long."

I nod along, agreeing with him. She is a good cabin, and she didn't deserve to be alone this long.

"I don't mean to pry, but that's my truck outside with the snow-plow. I can't help keeping myself busy, you know how it goes.

Anywho, I was clearing the road past your place, and I noticed a gold motorcycle pulling out. Must have been Sunday evening?"

"Mhm?" I respond, sipping my coffee.

"Well, I know you ain't from around here, so I was just wonderin' if someone was, uh, bothering you or anything."

I try to steady my face as his comment hits me like a stab in the heart. Samson wasn't bothering me. I liked him being around. Too much.

"No, nothing like that."

He just gave me the 12 Lays of Christmas, that's all.

"He had an issue with his bike."

Then he fucked me into the dirt out in the woods.

"He used my tools and headed back out once it was safe."

He called me his little toy and gave me some of the best orgasms of my life.

"Ahh, I see, I see, that's good," Vern replies. "You seem like a nice lady, so of course you'd help anyone that came to your door needing some help."

If only he knew how much I'd 'helped' Samson.

Vern looks down at his feet, shaking his head, before looking back up at me.

"Listen Mary, I reckon I should warn ya. That fella's not really the kind of company a lady such as you should be keepin'. He's only brought sin and corruption down on this county, is the truth of it."

"What do you mean?" I ask, suddenly very interested in what he has to say, while also souring on the judgmental old man.

"Well, I don't like to talk about this kind of stuff, I'm a Christian man and this is a Christian town after all. But, but that's the point! He's got strangers piling into this area by the carful, peddlin' his drugs and, and fornication materials and such. He's corruptin' this place slowly, but surely. Best you avoided all that."

A bit too late, buddy. The corruption has come and gone. *I* came, over and over.

"Well, thanks for the warning, Vern. I'll keep that in mind," I say with a big, fake smile. He nods his head, seemingly pleased with that.

"Alright, you do that. I'll let you get back to your lunch, Mary. Merry Christmas to ya. Mary, Merry! Ha!"

"Merry Christmas," I answer as he walks away with a wave.

I pull my phone back out as soon as he settles back into his booth, my heart racing.

"I own a couple businesses. One sells toys, one sells treats."

"You have good taste in sex toys, Mary. Expensive taste, too."

'It's a lot more rewarding, peddling pleasure.'

My mind races, going back over Samson's words.

"Holy fuck," I whisper to myself. No fucking way. I need to confirm my suspicions.

I plop a twenty on the table, overpaying for my meal, and walk straight over to the cottage. The door chimes as it opens and I pace the floor, waiting. The young biker walks out from the same curtain, travel mug in hand, yawning.

"You're back," he announces in surprise. "Didn't expect to see you again. You must've had a fun weekend," he says, presumably about the cookies.

Yeah, with your DAD!

Fuck.

He sips his coffee, watching me with interest.

My feet shift nervously. It still feels like Samson is a fantasy, like he only existed in our little bubble in the cabin. Preparing to speak his name to someone else makes me nervous, but I roll my shoulders back and do it anyway.

"Umm, this might be a weird question, but uh, is Samson here?"

He eyes me suspiciously over the rim of his mug as he takes another big swig.

"No, he isn't. He isn't in here much. Leaves the place for me to run, mostly. He might own the place, but I manage it," he replies, shifting his posture proudly.

"Okay, no problem. I was just wondering. Umm, could you point me toward his toy store then?"

"Fuck," he mutters under his breath. "Damn, lady. Respect. You must really be looking for a good time."

Oh, he has no idea. Still, there's no suitable response to that, especially when the good time I'm seeking is with his dad.

"So…?"

"It's a good thirty-minute drive from here. It's called the Toy Chest. Follow the state road north about twenty miles and you'll see it on the right."

"Well, thanks," I tell him. "What's your name by the way?"

"Sam," he responds a bit warily. "But he calls me Junior. Listen, did Dad send you here to check in on me or something? He hasn't been in for a few days."

Sam. Junior. I think about everything that Samson told me about his relationship with his kids, and I almost want to hug the little punk and tell him not to give his old man a hard time.

"Nothing like that, Sam, I promise. Thanks."

My fingers feel twitchy as I drive north. All the radio stations are playing Christmas music, and I feel more and more ridiculous the closer I get to the Toy Chest. What am I doing? Will he even want to see me?

I'm on the outskirts of Henderson, the nearest town to the north, when I see a red building on the right. A large, illustrated sign sits above a metal awning. 'The Toy Chest' is painted on the sign in swooping white letters, but it isn't a cutesy, quaint thing like the Milk & Cookies sign. Oh, no. The words sit over a set of busty, porn star breasts belonging to an illustrated pin-up girl.

Peddling pleasure is right.

The door chimes as I walk in. Just like every other store two days before Christmas, they're playing Christmas music. Pretty hard to ignore my Santa kink when I'm thinking about *my* Santa *and* surrounded by dildos.

Sex toys line the long wall in front of me, and racks of lingerie sit to the left. All the other things you'd expect in an adult store sit on more racks and along the walls.

Toys and Treats.

"Samson, you naughty boy," I whisper to myself, "you are in so much trouble when I find you."

If you even want me to.

A stunning young woman with jet black hair and a face full of piercings walks up to me, her black lipstick surrounding a bright, white smile.

"Anything I can help you with today? Shopping for a Christmas present or something for yourself?" she asks in a kind, raspy voice.

Here goes nothing.

"Actually, this might be a strange request, but is Samson here?"

She laughs. "Not strange at all, he's the owner. You're lucky, though, you almost missed him. He's headed over to the community center any minute."

"Community Center?"

"Yeah," she answers, shaking her head with a laugh, but I don't get the joke. "You from around here?"

"No, just visiting. Why do you ask?"

"Well, this shop is popular with the locals, but not so popular with the officials. Gotta love the hypocrisy when those bastards send their assistants in here to pick up shit for their mistresses and then rail against us in the paper the next day." She takes a deep exhale. "Anyway, he tries to get involved, be an upstanding member of the community and all. I remind him we're in an unincorporated zone, so there's nothing they can do, but it doesn't matter. He wants everyone to like him. What can I do, ya know?"

"Yeah, I kind of do know," I respond, thinking this all sounds right, about Samson and small towns in general.

"Sorry, sometimes the rant just needs to get out. Not healthy to hold things in! But you didn't come here to hear about small town politics, did you?"

Man, I like her spark, I think to myself.

She slaps the counter with another big smile and walks toward a side door, yelling, "Dad! Someone's here asking for you!"

Dad. Of course.

I hear her dad's gravel in her charming, raspy voice that makes her sound like a Golden Girl stuck in a twenty-something body.

Samson's deep voice rumbles out from a stairwell to my right, "I'm fucking busy, Sawyer!"

"Fine, you grumpy bastard! I'll tell the lady you're too busy to speak to a SMOKIN' HOT woman standing in your fucking sex shop!" she shouts, shaking her head. "Hopeless," she mumbles under her breath.

"Sawyer! What did you just say?!"

"You heard me, old man! Your ears still work!"

"Fucking hell, I'm fifty-five, not ninety! Hold on, hold on, I'm coming."

I stand by the counter, chuckling to myself at the interaction between Samson and his daughter. When he told me he put good people in charge of his stores, I hadn't realized that those good people were his kids. It does something inside my chest, thinking about that.

"However you know him, I'm sorry," Sawyer laughs. "He's bossy and grumpy, but he's a softie under it all."

"I heard that," Samson grumbles at Sawyer as he stomps down the stairs into the store. Our eyes meet, and I immediately break out into uncontrollable laughter. His brow furrows in response and he sets his hands on his hips, waiting for me to get it out of my system.

"You have GOT to be kidding me," I spit out between fits of laughter.

Samson is in a full Santa costume, his black biker boots the only thing giving him away. He even has a fur-trimmed white hat on.

"Yeah, yeah, yuck it up," Samson growls at me as I continue laughing.

When his deep voice sends a rush of wet heat to my core, I roll my eyes at myself. The Santa kink is certifiably undeniable.

"You done yet?" he asks, raising his left brow. His stern look makes his outfit look even more ridiculous, setting off another peal of laughter.

"You've got fifteen minutes before there's a toddler mutiny at the community center, Dad," Sawyer tells him as she slaps the counter again and disappears up the back stairs.

Samson walks right up to me, his spicy, woodsy scent and deep blue eyes immediately overwhelming my senses.

"Toys and treats?" I ask him with a smile, pinching his big bicep underneath the velvety red jacket.

"Vague, but true," he responds with a chuckle.

"You're a naughty, naughty man, Samson Nicholas."

"You already knew that, Mary. Now what are you doing in my shop? If you're buying shit for some other guy, then I'm sorry to tell you, but we're out of whatever it is. Everything. Sold out of everything."

My cheeks go pink. "Jealousy doesn't suit you, St. Nick."

"Oh, I see. You're buying yourself a new battery operated dick because you miss me. Got it." He winks. "Sorry, but there's no substitution. The only thing in the store that'll do it isn't for sale," he says with a sly smirk.

"DAD! TIME!" Sawyer yells down the stairs.

"She's a bossy little thing," Samson says with a proud smile.

"No idea where she could have gotten that from," I tease, and he gives me a playful pinch of his own.

"Seriously, what's up, little toy? Be a good girl and tell me why you're here."

Another flood of arousal courses through me.

"I've been thinking about things. Deciding about things, actually. About what I want."

"And? Do you have a list for Santa?"

"Not a list, just a request."

"Tell me, little toy. Don't be greedy, the kids are waiting for Santa."

"Well, that's just it. I think I've been waiting, too. Waiting a long time for something to wake me up. You did that. Ever since you left the cabin, I've been greedy for more. I'm not used to that. For the past two years, I thought all the things I wanted were in the past, but there *is* more for me. You taught me that. And when I think about what I want, it's more of this. More of you. I want *you*. I want you to have me, for more than a rental."

Samson smiles, letting me pull him into me by the lapels of his Santa coat. I thread my fingers through the strands of his white hair, then down his cheek, feeling his beard scratch against my skin.

"I want you too, angel. Since the first night, if I'm being honest. But I needed to let you decide for yourself what *you* wanted. Life's forced too many things on you. I didn't want to be another one." He leans in and spreads my lips open with his tongue, demanding entrance like he owns my mouth. He does.

I'm not scared to give myself to him, because I know I have so much more to give. It's good that I took the time to grieve, because now I feel ready to go into the world and latch on to the things that make me feel vibrant and alive.

I'd want Will to do that if I were gone. I'd want him to reach his hands out into the world and take every good thing he could grasp. I'd want him to shine so brightly that I could see him from my place in the stars.

Samson and I stand in the middle of his toy store holding on to each other until the sound of a throat clearing makes us both turn to the side.

"Thank fuck for whatever this is," Sawyer says with a cheeky smile, "but if the point of this whole Santa thing is to make the community like you, then not showing up is probably going to have the opposite effect."

"I told you she's smarter than me," Samson murmurs with a proud smile. "Sawyer, this is my girlfriend, Mary," he says as he looks down toward me, the question glimmering in his eyes. *Girlfriend.* A smile spreads across my face as I nod. I like the sound of that. "Mary, this is my daughter Sawyer."

"We already met, Dad. I told you; she's smokin' hot." She turns to me, one hand on her hip. "Mary, it's nice to meet you. Now, if you have any influence on this insufferable man, can you please get him out of my store?"

"Your store, huh? Interesting." Samson says with a curl of his lip. "Mary, do you want me to meet you at your cabin for dinner? I can bring takeout or pick up stuff to make something, whatever you want."

"What? Are you kidding? And miss you playing Santa? No way. I'm coming. Do you need a Mrs. Clause to accompany you? Or an elf, maybe?"

Samson gives me a dangerous, playful look. "The only outfits I have for that are on that rack over there," he states, pointing to a rotating display full of Christmas themed lingerie, lubes, and toys. Everything on the rack reads more 'strip club' than 'community center'.

"Yeah, on second thought, I'll just watch you from the back," I laugh. "I will take *these*, though," I tell him as I grab a candy cane shaped vibrator, reindeer tail butt plug, peppermint tingling lube, and a Mrs. Clause outfit. "For later. You can put these on your tab, Mr. Clause."

"Sooooo much more than I needed to know. Thanks for that, Mary," Sawyer says, imitating a gag as she walks behind the counter and smiles again. "Nice to meet you, though. I hope to see you around."

"You too," I call out as I take Samson's hand to walk outside.

"I like her," I tell him as I drop my Christmas goodies in my trunk. Samson comes up behind me, circling his arms around me in a warm hug.

"And I like you," he tells me, kissing along my neck and tickling me with his scratchy beard, "a lot. My greedy little toy." He shuts my new collection of presents in the trunk and spins me around for a kiss.

"Ride with me?" he whispers in my ear, setting off a trail of goosebumps down my neck.

"I'd rather stay alive, thank you very much. There's a lot I want to live for. Other things I want to *ride*." I raise my eyebrows up twice for effect and he laughs, licking a trail up my neck to my ear and biting down on the lobe.

"Follow me," Samson says as he throws his leg over his motorcycle. "I'm going to make all your Christmas wishes come true."

He turns around with a wink and a bright, dangerous smile as he revs his engine, and then he's off down the road. I watch him as he drives away, his Santa hat blowing behind him.

"You already did."

The future has been a blank page for me for the last two years, but as I follow Samson to the community center, that page stops looking empty and starts looking ready to be filled. I take a deep inhale as a smile spreads across my face, feeling so grateful to be alive. I think of all the things I want to experience, a Christmas list of life left to live, and I feel greedy with desire to experience it all.

THE END

ACKNOWLEDGMENTS

There's no other place to start than with my husband. You consistently believe in me even (and especially) when I don't believe in myself. You're equally good at listening to me complain and offering suggestions (when I agree to hear them). I know it's a massive burden to be my primary reader for all of my spice scenes, but you do it with grace, poise, and delicious facial expressions/shocked laughter that my needy ego has come to crave. I'd pick you every time.

As the mother of young children, writing my first two books has been the first big thing I've done all for myself in about 8 or 9 years. What I didn't expect was the pride and support my children have offered me this year as I write. My son even told the cashier at Barnes and Noble that his mom was a new author, and they were both so excited for me that it makes me emotional just thinking about it. I'm so grateful for their support.

Don't even get me started on my fur baby, the sweetest, gentlest, softest friend I've ever had. There's no amount of stress that petting her velvety little head can't solve.

To my mom- I'm grateful that you didn't hide your Fabio cover historical romances very well. I don't think I would have gotten this far without reading about the Dukes and Pirate Kings and naughty rakes in those books. I know a lot of authors worry about their moms reading what they write, and I'm very grateful that I feel the exact opposite.

I'm also grateful to the rest of my family- my sister, my in laws, aunts, cousins, grandma, etc. who have been so kind and supportive about my book.

My sincere gratitude to the lovely, kind, strange, wonderful staff at

Firefly for keeping me caffeinated and giving me a place to write words. I felt welcomed the first day I walked in, and that has morphed into a feeling of friendship and support that has meant so much on my good writing days and my bad. I know that a rice krispie treat isn't breakfast, but thank you for never making me feel bad for ordering one at 8:20 a.m.

Thank you to my Bookstagram fam for your support. The writing world can be harsh and intense, but you'd never know that in my little corner of social media. I'm so grateful to be able to talk books with such a delightful group of readers, and especially thankful for your encouragement of my writing. It means a ton, and I promise to keep you stocked up with smutty book recommendations. I'll make you all read monster smut if it kills me, and then I'll haunt you until you do.

Big thanks to my developmental editor, Theryn Jo Wolfe, for taking on this project. You understood what I wanted to do with this story from the start. This book would not be anywhere near what it is without your guidance and suggestions. Someone has to be the one to tell me, "most people wouldn't immediately tell all their deepest secrets to a strange man who showed up at their doorstep at night", and I'm glad you were the one to break it to me.

Penultimately, and I mean this sincerely, I don't think this book would exist without my beta reader, line editor, and proofreader Alyx Ramos. You're the first person other than my husband to read my writing, and your enthusiastic support and generosity with your time and feedback was the first time I really thought I could actually do this; I could really release a book. You always tell me what a fan you are of my writing, and I want you to know what a fan I am of yours as well. Please keep working with me forever, I need you.

Finally, thank YOU for taking a chance on this book. I'm so excited to release my smut baby into the world, and I sincerely hope it jingles your bells. If you liked this book, stick with me, because my idea journal is bursting at the seams with more spicy fun.

ABOUT THE AUTHOR

Oona Grace is an emerging author of high spice romance. This is Oona's first book.

Oona Grace is a voracious reader of smutty romance who decided to fulfill her dream of writing her own novels. She subscribes to the philosophy of *"Write the smut you wish to see in the world"*, filling her stories with relatable, flawed, endearing characters with quick wits and dirty minds.

Oona lives in the Midwestern United States and only regrets that fact from approximately January through April. When she's not reading or writing, Oona spends time with her two children, husband, and dog. She loves to travel and has lived in Japan, Scotland, and England.

Follow Oona on Social Media:
    Instagram @oonagraceauthor
    TikTok @authoroonagrace

ALSO BY OONA GRACE

All In His Head

Coming May 2023

Head to the next page for a sneak peek of the first draft of Chapter 1 of All In His Head

Preorder on Amazon

ALL IN HIS HEAD

CHAPTER 1

GABE

It's Tuesday morning, and I woke up handcuffed to a wall. I'm lying on a dingy mattress in only my boxers, covered in blood. My phone alarm is blaring, and my heart rate is rapidly escalating. None of this makes any sense.

I pull on the cuffs, which are solidly attached to hooks embedded in the drywall. I check myself for injuries, not feeling anything specific, but there's blood on my hands and smeared across my abdomen.

The room is a mess, covered in clothes, takeout boxes, and... cups. Why the hell are there so many cups? There's stuff everywhere, thrown around haphazardly in a way that makes my brain hurt. My eyes keep scanning the room for any clues, and I land on a cheap desk in the corner.

The scratched wooden desk holds half a dozen various mugs and plastic tumblers, some hard seltzer and mini wine bottles, papers, books, and a curling iron. There's a mirror next to the desk, one of those tall body-length ones, leaning against the wall. It has pictures of smiling girls taped along its edges. Am I in a woman's room? Are women this messy, or is this some kind of holding room?

I'd be embarrassed to say that I don't know what a woman's bedroom looks like, but now is not the time to delve into my issues with women. Still, I wince, hoping no one actually lives here.

There's probably a smarter way to handle a hostage situation, but since my phone alarm is still blaring and my brain doesn't start functioning until after my second cup of coffee, I just start yelling.

"Hello? Anybody there? I'm locked up in here!"

I'm quiet then, listening as best as I can over the alarm. I think I hear a noise down the hall. It sounds like an entire junk drawer spilling onto the floor.

"Shit. I'm coming!"

The voice calling out is from a woman. Most people would probably be relieved, but my fear of talking to a strange woman is almost deeper than my fear of being handcuffed in a dirty room. She chuckles as she walks down the hall, her voice getting closer.

"I'm coming!" She laughs. "Sound familiar? You heard it enough times last night."

She opens the door with a yawn and looks at me with a genuine, sleepy smile, but it quickly wilts when she sees the panic on my face.

"Whoops. I forgot to let you out of the handcuffs, my bad."

She crosses the room quickly and grabs my phone from the side of the bed, disabling the alarm. The room is quiet now, but my pulse is roaring as she kneels on the mattress and starts freeing my wrists. I hear Velcro ripping apart as she frees my right arm. The handcuffs were Velcro? What kind of handcuffs are Velcro?

She reaches across me, wearing just a camisole and undies, and I freeze. I can't breathe as her large, soft left breast brushes across my neck and chin. She's reaching over to undo my left wrist restraint, but she's short and small, minus her chest. I shift from anxiety to panic as she sinks further into me to reach the hook on the wall. She takes the end of the Velcro strap and pulls, releasing my other wrist.

"All set! Free as a bird."

She pushes forward off her knees, crawling over me to sit next to me on the bed. I wonder if I slap myself hard enough, would I wake up from this dream? This can't be real life.

Handcuffs, blood, and half-naked women might be a normal way to wake up in an action movie, but none of them fit into the life of Gabe Amante, writing center tutor and semi-professional avoider of women.

I hear my father's voice echo in my head, preaching to the congregation in my small hometown about sin and temptation. I imagine him berating me for the sin of noticing what my captor is wearing, admonishing me for not totally hating how her breast felt pushed up against me. I remember what happened the last time I followed a woman into a bedroom. Shadows swirl as panic attacks me from both the past and the present.

I sneak a glance at this girl as I stand up, frantically scanning the room for my clothes. She's a petite brunette with the athletic body of a gymnast. Muscular thighs lead up to small cotton briefs, with a hint of abs peeking out between the top of her undies and the hem of her cami. She's visibly strong despite her compact, curvy frame.

Christ, what am I doing? Stop looking at her body and focus, Gabe. I force my eyes up to her face, hoping she didn't notice me staring at her body. My eyes track her movements in case she's dangerous. She had me locked up in here, after all.

She looks slightly younger than me, twenty or twenty-one maybe? Probably a student at State. Her face is cherubic, but there's something mischievous underneath. At six-feet-one. I'm almost a foot taller than her, but between her muscles and the whole 'waking up as her bloody prisoner' thing, I'm not going to risk underestimating her.

I have a decent amount of lean muscle from my daily calisthenics routine, but I don't know how to fight. Blinking several times, I clear the thoughts about her body away- I have to focus on getting out of here. My clothes sit piled by the door, so I shuffle over to put them on. She's watching me, staring at my and it makes me nervous.

"What's with all the cups?" I ask. Of all the things I could ask, I ask about the cups. What the fuck, Gabe?

"Eh, it's an ADHD thing. I bring 'em in here and forget to take 'em out. There's no dopamine hit from basic cleaning tasks. It's a problem I have."

One of many, I think to myself. Not that I can judge.

"Listen," I tell her, my eyes pleading, "I don't know what happened here, but whatever it is, you've got the wrong guy."

I slip into my first pant leg, stumbling with nerves. I trip down into the mattress while trying to keep an eye on her. For safety purposes, obviously. Not because she's an adorable half-dressed woman. That might sound like sarcasm, but it isn't. I really don't think about women like that. I turned that part of me off a long time ago.

She looks me over with an expression I can't comprehend, then smirks and stretches her arms over her head, relaxing into the bed like a lazy, satisfied cat.

"No, you're the right guy. I definitely got what I was looking for. You're quite the screamer. I love being fully in control like that." She smiles again and reaches toward me, playfully pinching my nipple.

I gasp, lurching forward and scrambling to pull my pants up and move away from her.

What happened last night? Why is she admitting to torturing me? Does this tiny college town have some kind of gymnast mafia?

I'm threading my belt through the loops, missing half of them with how shaky my hands are. Why am I even worrying about my damn belt? I need to get out of here ASAP.

I look back over at her and she's quietly laughing at me like I'm pathetic- which I am. The first time in five years that I'm alone with a woman in her room, and she's some psycho criminal. My track record is impressively bad.

"Miss, I'm confused. I don't know why you did all this to me," I say questioningly, motioning towards the blood on my lower abs and pelvis and then holding out my bloody hands for her to see. I still can't tell where the blood came from, but at least it seems like I'm not bleeding anymore.

She grimaces and then holds her palms up, shrugging her shoulders."Yeah, sorry about that. Couldn't be helped, given the situation and all. I told you what was happening, you know, *down there.* You didn't seem to mind though, it almost seemed like you were into it.

You told me you 'like it messy'. Not all guys can handle that kinda thing. I was impressed." She shrugs again as she walks to her desk and starts shoving things aside, looking for something.

The thought strikes me that she might be searching for a weapon, but before I can react she turns around and hands me a pack of wipes.

"They're makeup wipes, but they should clean you up ok."

I take one out and scrub my stomach, still wholly confused. It makes absolutely no sense that I'd be better at handling torture than the usual criminals she roughs up. My frustration rises the longer we talk. I need to get out of this house before things get any more bizarre.

She watches me scrub my skin. "Look, Richard, I'm sorry if last night was too much for you. It was just some handcuffs, and I know I smacked you around a bit, but I thought we were on the same page. I thought we wanted the same things."

I'm sweating now, my mind is swimming. The wipes have done a decent job on the blood, but my skin feels sticky and wrong. I can't think straight. Everything she says confuses me more and more. I haven't even had my morning coffee to get my brain to start braining properly.

She takes my phone from the bed and hands it to me. I check the time as I slip it into my pocket. Shit. It's seven a.m. on a Tuesday. I have work today, and if I don't get out of here immediately, I'm going to be late. How is this my life?

I grab my shirt from the ground to throw it on. My frustration flows as I throw it over my head, and I snap.

"On the same page? We aren't even in the same book! I'm not Richard, I don't know what happened here, and I absolutely don't want any part of this- the blood, the handcuffs, the torture. I'm a good person. This isn't who I am. I just want to get out of here. I won't tell anyone, ok? I won't call the police. Just please let me leave."

Whatever word vomit I just spewed was the wrong thing to say. The twinkle of mischief in her eyes morphs into a blaze of fury, and it scares the shit out of me. I can barely maintain eye contact with a female barista to take my coffee order, let alone handle this woman's intense glare.

It took me months of effort to even chat with my female coworker,

Scarlett, and if I'm being honest, that still makes me nervous. I have no frame of reference for what to do when I've got the pissed-off eyes of a tiny mafia gymnast boring holes into my skull.

Her voice is pure venom now, and I step back towards the door as she stalks towards me.

"What the fuck do you mean, call the police? Over what? Some light kink? You know, I've had men sneak out of my room, but I've never had someone so blatantly disrespect me over what I choose to do with my body. What WE did!"

She stops and points at me like I'm the criminal here.

"You think you're some good guy? Well, you're not. Actually, you're worse than most. I'm sorry it was 'torture' to spend the night with me, but complaining about some blood? Grow the fuck up. I'm not letting some random asshole shame me over my own bodily functions, or the activities he consented to. Get the hell out of my house!"

I scramble out of the room in pure panic, barreling through the front door. As soon as my feet hit the porch, cold and misted with morning dew, I realize I'm barefoot. I'm standing there, thinking about my next move, when a sneaker flies at me and pelts me in the forehead. The other one lands square in my sternum with a reverberating thud. I raise my hands defensively, but I only have two shoes and the attack is over.

"You better hope you never see me again, or I'll let everyone know exactly who you really are!"

She slams the door shut, leaving me alone on the porch with a blooming goose egg on my forehead and questions I'm not sure I'll ever be able to answer.

As I step into my shoes, I'm left wondering who exactly this girl thinks I am, and if she did figure me out, what am I? After two dozen years of life, all I know myself to be is a collection of fears, failures, and things I don't want out of life.

I step off the porch and try to forget the events of this morning, adding whatever the hell happened here to my list of things I never want to do again.

Printed in Great Britain
by Amazon

16022968R00082